> **"In Denmark we say that aquavit is strong as a Viking, fiery as a lover, cold as an iceberg and fresh as a virgin."**

He reached across and took her unresisting hand in his own, lacing his fingers through hers. "Together you and I could generate the power of aquavit, I believe. For me the strength and passion—for you the ice and freshness, *ja?*"

"There is no you and I," she said, denying the hypothesis vehemently, "nor could there ever be."

"You don't believe in fairy tales, then?"

"Of course not! Does anyone?"

"Perhaps you'll find your own happy ending where you least expect it."

Dear Reader,

We know from your letters that many of you enjoy
traveling to foreign locations—especially from the
comfort of your favorite chair. Well, sit back, put your
feet up and let Harlequin Presents take you on a yearlong
tour of Europe. Postcards from Europe will feature a
special title every month, set in one of your favorite
European countries, written by one of your favorite
Harlequin Presents authors. This month, discover
Denmark and, in particular, Copenhagen. The city is the
center of Danish government and home to nearly a third
of the country's population. And, as you're about to find
out, it's also a city with a fairy-tale atmosphere that
makes it the perfect setting for a love affair!

The Editors

P.S. Don't miss the fascinating facts we've compiled
about Denmark. You'll find them at the end of the story.

HARLEQUIN PRESENTS

Postcards from Europe

1619—THE ALPHA MAN by Kay Thorpe
1628—MASK OF DECEPTION by Sara Wood
1636—DESIGNED TO ANNOY by Elizabeth Oldfield
1644—DARK SUNLIGHT by Patricia Wilson
1650—THE BRUGES ENGAGEMENT by Madeleine Ker
1660—ROMAN SPRING by Sandra Marton
1668—YESTERDAY'S AFFAIR by Sally Wentworth
1676—SUDDEN FIRE by Elizabeth Oldfield
1684—THE TOUCH OF APHRODITE by Joanna Mansell
1691—VIKING MAGIC by Angela Wells
1700—NO PROMISE OF LOVE by Lilian Peake
1708—TOWER OF SHADOWS by Sara Craven

ANGELA WELLS

Viking Magic

Harlequin Books

TORONTO • NEW YORK • LONDON
AMSTERDAM • PARIS • SYDNEY • HAMBURG
STOCKHOLM • ATHENS • TOKYO • MILAN
MADRID • WARSAW • BUDAPEST • AUCKLAND

ISBN 0-373-11691-8

VIKING MAGIC

Copyright © 1993 by Angela Wells.

This edition published by arrangement with Harlequin Enterprises B. V.

® and TM are trademarks of the publisher. Trademarks indicated with ® are registered in the United States Patent and Trademark Office, the Canadian Trade Marks Office and other in countries.

Printed in U.S.A.

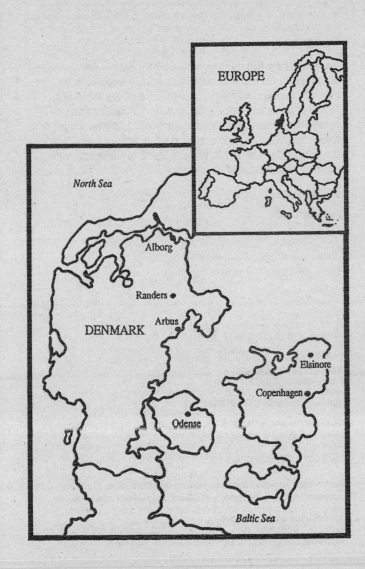

Dear Reader,

I immediately fell in love with Copenhagen—its combination of old and new, its parks, bronze statues and, of course, the romantic ambience of the fabulous Tivoli amusement park with its colorful landscaping, excellent entertainment and variety of restaurants. Quiet canals and easy access to surrounding villages and the beaches of the Danish Riviera, helped to make my visit there an unforgettable experience.

Enjoy!

Angela Wells

Books by Angela Wells

HARLEQUIN PRESENTS
1164—LOVE'S WRONGS
1181—ERRANT DAUGHTER
1492—TATTERED LOVING
1581—RECKLESS DECEPTION

HARLEQUIN ROMANCE
3143—SUMMER'S PRIDE
3167—ENDLESS SUMMER
3246—TORRID CONFLICT

CHAPTER ONE

Every man's life is a fairy-tale
written by God's fingers.
H. C. Andersen

IF IT hadn't been for the capricious whim of her
younger sister she would have been hard at work in
London at this moment. Instead she was gazing
sombrely out of the window of a smart Mercedes taxi
as it left behind the flat landscaped suburbs of the
island of Amager, crossing the bridge to the main
island of Zealand and the approach to the city of
Copenhagen.

Gina settled back in the comfortable upholstery and
expelled her breath in a gesture of resignation. Until
Margaret's frantic visit four days earlier she'd resolved
to apply herself assiduously to her job in an attempt to
exorcise Marcus Pritchard from her memory entirely,
and Denmark had meant nothing to her except as a
dark finger of land on a map pointing upwards into the
North Sea.

How strange it still seemed to call her mother by her
forename, a practice suggesting an intimacy that was
far from existing! Yet for as long as she could remember she'd been instructed to do so. As a child it had
been embarrassing and as both teachers and playmates
had looked askance at the familiarity she'd reverted to
the ubiquitous 'Mum' in their presence, but woe betide
her if she had lapsed into this form of address in
Margaret's presence!

Now, of course, she knew her mother had been too

7

vain to acknowledge a daughter whose age would be an indication of her own. Then, it had added another stamp of 'difference' on a child whose father rarely appeared in the family home and who spent most of her free time in the company of paid supervisors.

Now, as the taxi proceeded on its uninterrupted journey beneath a blue veil of a sky flocked with white clouds, she felt her natural curiosity nudged into wakefulness, and leaned forward to obtain a better view of the wide tree-lined road with its four carriageways for motor traffic and its two bicycle lanes, intrigued despite her earlier uninterest.

Beautifully restored façades of the older buildings melded with the elegant lines of the newcomers standing shoulder to shoulder; hotels nestled against glittering jewellery stores, elegant fur shops stood adjacent to brightly lit American-style fast-food bars, and fashion boutiques vied with the eye-catching displays of porcelain and glass in neighbouring shop windows.

To her surprise a few minutes later the taxi pulled up outside a fashion shop in one of the main city streets as the driver indicated she had reached her destination. Alighting hesitantly, she cast anxious eyes around her, wondering just where her hotel was, as she paid him the exact amount on the meter, feeling strangely guilty as she refrained from adding a tip in accordance with the multi-lingual notice in the cab. Accustomed to living and working in the United Kingdom, where it was customary to tip taxi drivers, she felt uncomfortably mean.

Certainly the driver seemed satisfied enough, she accorded with relief as with a smile he pointed to an illuminated notice indicating that her hotel was at the end of a narrow passageway leading from the main street. Grasping her small suitcase in one hand, Gina followed the sign, drawing up with a soft exclamation of pleasure as she found herself in an oblong courtyard surrounded on two sides by what was obviously her hotel, a tall building of nineteenth-century architecture, its red-tiled roof gabled and decorated with iron curlicues, its many-paned white-framed windows set in mellowed red brick reflecting the pale northern sunshine.

To her right the blind yellowstone wall of another tall building rose majestically—a perfect backdrop for the dozen or so pink-clothed tables, laid for morning coffee, their pristine china no whiter than the latticed chairs which surrounded them. Beneath her feet large paving slabs formed a diamond pattern, while above her head stiff-framed sun umbrellas cast their shadows over half a dozen or so people enjoying the quiet scene. Round-headed bay trees stood stiffly in their pots, while from low white troughs scarlet geraniums and royal blue lobelia spilled haphazardly towards the ground.

Inside the reception hall she found a tiny antiquated lift barely large enough to take herself, her suitcase and a bellboy to her fifth-floor room. Aware that the Danes were famous for their elegant designs and their 'down comforters' she wasn't surprised to find her single bed covered by a thick duvet quilt, or to discover the fitted furniture was simply but efficiently styled.

What brought her to a standstill was the realisation that her bedroom was under the eaves, so that the walls angled sharply towards the ceiling, lending the room a special character. Sliding open the door to the en-suite bathroom, she was faced with a room every line and angle of which was tiled in glistening white and amply provided with mirrors, giving the impression of a chapel carved out of snow.

She was being fanciful, she chided herself, long distant memories of the fairy-tales of Hans Christian

Andersen stirring in her mind. It was absurd to imagine that a modern city could still evoke that kind of magic! Moving to the double-glazed dormer windows by her bed, she threw both panes open, to be rewarded by a vista of church spires, each one different in design yet each unmistakably decorated by copper strips and inlays, greened with age and atmosphere. Beneath her lay the vista of the outdoor restaurant in its sheltered patio. Despite the fact that she was only yards from the main street, not one sound of the flowing traffic penetrated the stillness. The double glazing was to prevent the penetration of winter cold rather than noise pollution, she concluded.

Unpacking took only minutes. Uncertain of the kind of climate which awaited her, she'd consulted her hastily purchased travel guide, to be informed that Copenhagen was on the same latitude as Newcastle-on-Tyne in England and shared similar weather patterns. Consequently she'd prepared for the worst while hoping for the best. It wasn't, she reminded herself sternly, as she tucked her rose-printed nylon nightdress beneath the quilt, as if this was a holiday. She was here on a mission, and the sooner she set out on it the better! Hopefully she would find Suzie and talk some reason into her head within the six days she had allotted herself.

Still dressed in the chestnut-coloured cotton suit with its pleated skirt and casual blouse-type jacket over a short-sleeved white silk top in which she had travelled, she dragged a comb through her wavy dark hair, tucking the long side strands behind her ears, before renewing the soft bronze lipstick which emphasised the gentle curves of her soft-lipped mouth.

Trained in a business where presentation was paramount, she had long since learned the best way to project the image of herself she wished other people to see. As far as Marcus had been concerned she had succeeded too well, she admitted as she paid cursory attention to the long dark lashes fringing her clear grey eyes. What he had seen, he hadn't got! The veneer of sophistication, her throw-away attitude of *laissez-faire*, had deceived him into believing she had shared his own amoral values.

For that, she was entirely to blame, and his reaction to the discovery that beneath the hard shell of assumed glamour there lurked a conventional nature had been no more than she deserved. Unfortunately, being able to accept responsibility for what had happened didn't make her feel any better about it!

Suppressing a sigh, she surveyed the map of Copenhagen with which she'd already armed herself before leaving England, refreshing her memory as to the location of the street where Suzie's presence had last been authenticated.

A frown of exasperation lined her brow as she shook her dark head in bewilderment. How could her young sister have behaved so inconsiderately? However fraught the relationship with their mother, how could she have cared so little for the older woman as to send notice of her intentions through another teenager?

'She wanted to go to this pop festival at Roskilde in Denmark,' Margaret Price had explained tonelessly the evening she'd arrived on Gina's doorstep in obvious distress. 'I thought perhaps things would be better if we had some time away from each other, so I agreed, even though it meant her taking time off from school before the end of term. It's not as if they get much study done the last week or so anyway.' She'd made a helpless gesture with one beautifully manicured hand. 'I knew the two other girls she was going with. It all seemed so simple. . .'

Simple it hadn't been! Because when Wendy and

Laura had returned they'd brought a verbal message from Suzie to the effect that she'd met a Danish boy and had no intention of returning to England to complete her studies.

Margaret had been close to tears as she'd responded to her elder daughter's terse demand for further information—a phenomenon in itself, as Gina knew her mother rarely allowed emotion to disturb the still beautiful contours of her face.

'The boy's name is Svend,' she'd declared. 'Apparently he's a twenty-year-old student. When I insisted on more information Wendy gave me the address of a flat in Copenhagen where they'd stayed—the three girls, this Svend and two other boys. It seems their relationship was so informal they didn't even bother to exchange surnames,' she added bitterly, before thrusting a slip of paper into Gina's hands and continuing bleakly, 'Wendy wrote down the address of the flat for me. Apparently it belongs to this boy Svend because it was he who suggested they go to Copenhagen instead of staying on in Roskilde when the pop festival ended.' She paused, making a helpless gesture with both hands. 'The problem is there's no point my going over there. Suzie hates me. . .we were barely on speaking terms the week before she left. She'd turn and run if she set eyes on me. . .but I thought. . .'

Gina gazed down at the map unseeingly, her mind preoccupied with the unhappy little scene in her own living-room. She hadn't had to be psychic to determine Margaret's thoughts. Her mother had known she had no immediate plans to go on holiday and had assumed she would be free to chase after Suzie. What Margaret hadn't known were the twin reasons for her decision to immerse herself in work: her need to occupy each waking moment with creative thought so that she had no time to dwell on Marcus's sudden vitriolic departure from her life, and the struggle for economic survival which was facing the advertising agency where she was employed.

Of course, her mother had been right. There was no way she could have turned her back on Suzie: charming, vivacious, affectionate Suzie. Spoiled and wilful she might be at times, but the emotional distance between them caused by the difference in their ages and their forced separation in childhood had slowly been closing over the past two years. Their mother was right. If anyone could persuade Suzie to give up her madcap scheme it would be she, Gina.

However, getting to Denmark had proved more difficult than she'd anticipated. Rather naïvely, she'd imagined most flights would be heading for the summer sun. It had been the girl in the travel agency who had put her right about that!

'Copenhagen could be tricky, what with two trade conventions and the music festival.'

'Oh!' For a moment Gina had been nonplussed. 'I thought the music festival was over?'

'You mean the pop concert at Roskilde?' The other girl had smiled. 'Sure, that's over, but the Copenhagen Summer Festival is in full swing in July and the international jazz festival has just started. What with the music and the conventions, the place is bursting at the seams—but we'll do our best for you.'

Rather chastened, she'd taken the seat indicated while the travel consultant had tracked down flights via her VDU, gratefully accepting the more expensive club class when nothing cheaper proved available. Even finding hotel accommodation had proved difficult. Obviously she'd been lucky in what the travel agency had found for her, she thought approvingly as she glanced round the attractive room. Still, since time was at a premium, she couldn't afford to waste it admiring her surroundings. In the circumstances, the sooner she started on Suzie's trail, the better it would be! Refolding the map neatly, she slipped it into her jacket pocket.

Whether it was the relaxed ambience of the city, the clear warm air, or a strange sense of anticipation which heightened all her senses, Gina couldn't be sure, but as she made her way towards the Rådhuspladsen—the imposing City Hall square—measuring her stride to avoid the rows of cobblestones which checkered the paving stones beneath her feet, she suddenly felt hungry, despite the champagne breakfast she'd enjoyed on the flight.

Enticed by the exotic smells issuing from a nearby many-storeyed building, she crossed the threshold to find herself on the ground floor of a gourmet's paradise. Small sets of tables and chairs surrounded open-style serveries offering an enormous variety of ethnic foods. Entranced by the selection, she wandered towards the centre of the complex to gaze upwards at tiers of galleries strung with lights, climbing plants and even trees. Torpedo-shaped glass lifts offered noiseless access to the different levels, on one of which a pianist sat at a grand piano playing classical music while an enormous golden pendulum suspended from the roof swung slowly from one side of the atrium to the other.

Danish cuisine wasn't anything to which she had ever given much thought before but 'when in Denmark'. . . The delicious aroma of small deep-fried meatballs persuaded her to choose the *frikadeller* served with sweet and sour cucumber, red cabbage and crisply fried potato chips, washed down with a glass of ice-cold Danish beer. Not a dish for a dieter, she allowed, but it was a long time since she'd enjoyed anything quite so much. Besides, she'd lost enough weight in the past weeks since she had walked out on Marcus not to have to worry about her seams splitting after the odd indulgence!

It was getting on for two in the afternoon as she crossed the Rådhuspladsen on her way towards the old part of the town. Here the bustle of the centre was muted, the roads narrow between the tall eighteenth-century buildings, each beautifully restored, the walls washed with shades of umber, rust and light blue. Rough cobbles teased her feet through the light soles of her shoes as she paused to stare down into basement antique shops and silver vaults, second-hand book-stores and small cosy cafés. Little wonder Suzie had fallen in love with this modern city which proudly displayed so much of its past—or was it the shadowy Svend who had really captured her sister's heart?

A pang of regret lanced through her as she recog-nised how little she still knew of Suzie's innermost feelings. Perhaps if the age-gap of eight years between them had been less. . .perhaps if she herself had stayed at home for a few years instead of finding separate lodgings as soon as she'd finished her A levels and joined Grantham and Marsh as a junior copywriter. . . She gave herself a mental shake. Sentiment would get her nowhere! In fact, it was a long time since she'd realised she was capable of such an emotion. For which Marcus must take the blame—or praise—depending on one's point of view, she accorded without bitterness.

For years she'd built up a protective shell around herself, a barrier against which the slings and arrows of outrageous fortune had bounced and fallen harmlessly to the ground. Her lips curved into an impulsive smile. Now there was an association of ideas—seeing her own situation in terms of Shakespeare's Prince of Denmark! Whatever the metaphor Marcus had changed all that. Bursting into her life with a devastating charm, he had undermined her defences with skill, until she had faced him as defenceless as a de-shelled crab, and he had destroyed her illusions with the cruel indifference of a natural predator.

So deep in thought had she been that she reached her destination before she'd made any definite plans about how to proceed. Making her way through large hooked-back wooden doors, she entered yet another courtyard. Unlike the one at the hotel, this was cobbled, one of the surrounding walls covered by some kind of vine while the whole was shaded by a large plane tree, beneath which six bicycles were chained. A wooden bench seat and a scatter of garden chairs suggested that the residents of the surrounding buildings might take their ease there on a summer's night.

Walking up three steps, she was soon in the foyer of the block of apartments she'd set out to find, and pressing the button in the lift which would take her to the top floor.

The building might be old, but this was no cheap accommodation, she observed as she stepped on to the landing. Close-fitted carpet on a well-lit passageway suggested the occupants were more affluent than the average student could be expected to be, unless of course he made a living from the less commendable pursuits some students were reputed to follow! Gina bit her lip. Now she was being over-dramatic. Perhaps Svend had generous parental support? Still, there was only one way to find out. She pressed a firm finger on the bell.

There was no answer. Impatience mingling with disappointment, she rang again, allowing her finger to dwell on the button for several seconds, determined to satisfy herself that the apartment was definitely unoccupied at the moment.

'*Ja!*'

'Oh!' A yelp of shock escaped her as the door opened

forcefully beneath her second assault to reveal a figure straight out of a Viking saga. Momentarily at a loss for words, her carefully prepared introductory speech departing to leave her mind a blank, she could only stare wide-eyed at the apparition before her.

Over six feet tall, naked save for a pair of blue and white striped boxer shorts, his frame athletically developed, the golden skin stretched in sleek, unblemished vitality over tautly developed muscles, the vision scowled at her, eyebrows flattened menacingly over eyes of the brightest, lightest blue she had ever seen.

Dear God! Please don't let this be Svend, she prayed. Instinct and an adolescence spent in observation rather than practice told her this was the kind of man who ate little girls like Suzie for breakfast. Besides, he was in no way the youth she had envisaged. This was Nordic Man in his prime. Her startled eyes absorbed the thick, short, golden-streaked hair swept back from a broad forehead, ears long and narrow as a satyr's which grew close to a beautifully formed skull, a mouth of unutterable sweetness countered by a long jaw carved out of golden teak faintly blurred by a light stubble, and a chin that jutted in a formidable challenge. Thirty or a little over if he was a day, and projecting all the self-assurance of years well used!

Her eyes dropped once more to the boxer shorts as embarrassed colour rose to her cheeks. Two-thirty in the afternoon and she had dragged him out of bed? It didn't need much imagination to guess that his presence there had been recreational rather than restitutional!

'*Hvad ønsker De?*'

The Danish eluded her but the tone of voice nearer a growl than a polite question suggested she was being asked to state her business. Perhaps she should offer to come back later? Hardly a practicable solution when she didn't even know if she could make herself under-

stood. Most Danes, she'd been assured by her guide
book, spoke excellent English. Being able to was not
the same as being willing to, however, and the icy glare
of the semi-nude man in front of her wasn't
encouraging.

'*Goddag.*' Forcing her mouth into a winsome smile,
Gina pronounced the greeting, so that it sounded like
the English 'good day', in accordance with the instructions of her Berlitz language guide. Not an easy tongue
to master at such short notice, but she had always felt
it was a basic courtesy for a tourist to make some
attempt, however feeble, to communicate in the tongue
of the host country. '*Taler De engelsk?*'

'Certainly.' Pellucid blue eyes never wavered from
their close scrutiny of her enquiring expression. 'Also
Swedish, Norwegian, Russian, German and Arabic.' A
certain smugness sugared his deep tones, making her
hackles rise.

Boastful, she judged unkindly, her instinctive disap-
proval of him strengthening. The kind of man who
kissed and told.

'If this is a survey, shouldn't you be writing down the
answers?' His mocking stare challenged her, his latent
hostility stirring her own adrenalin.

'I'm looking for someone called Svend.' She treated
his sarcasm with the contempt it deserved, unconsciously raising her chin in an attitude of defiance. 'I
understand he's known at this address? But, of course,
if it's an inconvenient moment to disturb you. . .?' She
hesitated delicately, one perfectly groomed eyebrow
slightly raised.

CHAPTER TWO

A QUICK encompassing movement of his light eyes absorbed every detail of her appearance from top to toe, before he stood back. 'What I was doing can always be continued later. I think you had better come in.'

'Thank you.' A small glow of triumph warmed her. At least he hadn't denied knowing Suzie's companion. Her initial surge of euphoria was instantly followed by dismay. On the other hand if Wendy had deliberately misled Margaret and *he* himself were Svend, her chances of winning her sister away from his wiles were slender to the point of anorexia. . .especially if it was Suzie who had been so recently in his arms. . . Youthful students were one thing, but if her impressionable sister had become involved with a man of this calibre. . .

Forcing herself to assume a composure she was far from feeling, Gina allowed him to usher her from the small lobby behind the front door into a living-room of graceful proportions. Her first impression was one of sunlight pouring in from the wall of windows facing her, casting bright patches across the fitted almond-green carpet. Mulberry-coloured curtains were fastened in strict discipline at the windows' extremities so that the view of attractive roofs and spires was uninterrupted.

Two black leather chesterfields faced each other across a low glass-topped table bearing a cylindrical flower vase of highly polished stainless steel surrounded by three slimmer and smaller cylinders of the same material, which, empty, could have been a rather large cruet set, but the true function of which was illustrated by the pure white candles, long and pointed, which emerged from their upper openings.

Stylish. . . Gina paused to pass her approving gaze around the rest of the room. She didn't need to read the manufacturer's name to recognise the sleek lines of a Bang and Olufsen television and VCR or its matching hi-fi and CD player stacked on a long, low teak drawer-unit. A shelf against one wall displayed a small collection of rainbow-hued glass bowls and ornaments in which colour flowed into colour in a multiform fantasy of design and chance. The forms were simple, graceful, unembellished by anything save the intensity of light and movement trapped in the glass itself. If she had to find fault it would be that the room was too perfect—too like an exhibition in some high-class furniture store. It betrayed nothing personal about its owner—unless he was an emotionless aesthete—and somehow she doubted that to be the case as her psyche responded to the presence of a simmering powerhouse within the lean, muscled frame before her.

Reluctantly she turned her eyes away, then gasped as her eyes fell on a painting in pride of place on the only wall at which she had not as yet glanced. A small exclamation of delight escaped her. Surely she wasn't mistaken. . .

'*Kom her*!'

As her breath caught in her throat, a strong hand fastened round her wrist, her unfriendly host commandeering both her body and attention. Even in Danish the brusque instruction was unmistakable as she was propelled across a threshold and with a fast movement of one strong arm sent revolving into a circle which ended when one of her calves struck the bed and she sat down heavily on its soft surface.

Dear heavens! She was in real trouble now. More adrenalin poured into her system, raising her pulse, sending the blood thundering through her veins as her face paled. 'No, wait! You have to listen to me. It's vitally important that I find my sister!'

Her anguish must have penetrated his obvious antagonism as, standing back, he gazed down at her, the prepossessing lines of his face softening slightly as a reluctant smile lifted the corners of his mouth.

'Relax, *min skat*, it's nearly a thousand years since our Danish King Canute possessed your English throne. We Danes have become reformed characters since then. It's no longer fashionable to pillage or plunder. . .or rape. Instead we spend our energies in hard work so that we can afford to pay our taxes and enjoy the benefits of a comfortable and well-ordered life.'

Cynicism glittered in the brightness of his light blue eyes as relief restored the colour to her cheeks, but her reprieve was short-lived as cynicism gave way to shrewdness. 'But I have to admit you confuse me. First you are looking for a man named Svend—then it is your sister. Do you suppose I run a rooming house, or can it be you are not so innocent as you appear? Shall we see?'

It sounded like a question, but he had no intention of waiting for her answer, as he dropped down on the bed beside her, lacing his fingers through her lustrous brunette tresses, controlling the movement of her head so she could not escape the seductive power of his mouth as he took her unwilling lips with practised artistry.

If she could have screamed she would have! But he was so close, his other hand pulling her hard against his naked chest, his face so near to her own that it was difficult for her to breathe—so difficult that she had to

open her mouth to draw in air only to find that he'd
taken advantage of the opportunity to deepen his kiss
into one of familiarity.

For a few seconds she was transfixed by the speed of
his action and the total unexpectedness of his assault
plus a shocked awareness that she was more mentally
revolted by his action than she was physically.

Sanity returned with the effect of an icy shower, as
she realised what was happening. She was in a strange
land with an even stranger man! With the sudden
strength of desperation she tore herself out of his now
relaxed embrace.

'Let me go!' Somehow she stumbled to her feet,
Suzie forgotten in the horror of the moment, as she
sought her own safety. 'How dare you assault me?'

'How dare you come here trying to put me off my
guard with some absurd story?' he countered with
simmering hostility, regarding her belligerent stance
with brooding interest. 'But my intention in bringing
you in here was never to enjoy the pleasure of your
body. I merely want to keep you where I can see you
while I dress more in accordance with entertaining an
unexpected caller. Although I admit to being intrigued
as to how far you were prepared to go to achieve your
ends.'

The man was infuriating with his blandness: the held-
back amusement, the implied accusation that she was
up to something nefarious.

'I don't understand your attitude.' Her hand rose to
her lips, soft and still tingling from the hard pressure
of his possessive mouth.

His gaze flickered as the movement registered and,
horrified at her own gesture of betrayal, Gina let her
hand fall to her side.

'You are interested in collectibles, *nej*?' The softly
voiced question was innocent of guile as he selected a

pair of black, jean-cut trousers from a built-in ward-robe and stepped into them with graceful and accurate power, as Gina struggled to control her erratic breathing.

Damn the man! How she would have loved to have seen him stumble like some lesser mortal. But his question was harmless, thankfully diverting.

'I admire lovely things,' she agreed cautiously. 'Why do you ask?'

There was a pause as he stretched his arms into the sleeves of a plain white T-shirt and pulled it over his head, powerful chest muscles expanding with animal efficiency.

'I noticed the way you—what is the word the Americans use? Cased? Yes, that is it, I think. I noticed the way you "cased my joint"!'

His English was superb, accentless and totally with-out the structured rhythm of some Scandinavian speech. The Americanism made Gina want to laugh, but there was something in those beautiful blue eyes with their clear, piercing quality which made her think better of it as they dwelt consideringly on her face.

'You have a very beautiful apartment,' she said stiffly. 'I'm sorry if you found my interest rude.'

'Gratifying,' he corrected softly. 'Tell me what you liked best—the Stelton steel perhaps? Or the Kosta Boda glass?'

Puzzled by his intensity but considerably more at ease now his lithe frame was effectively covered, Gina's hands fluttered in a gesture of indecision.

'They're both beautiful. . .'

'And the picture?' he prompted. 'That pleased you too?' Strong fingers snapped the catch at his waist, pulled the zip, tightened the leather belt above the sculpted curve of masculine hip.

'You mean the Knudsen?' It was impossible to hide

her excitement as his casual question seemed to confirm her first impression that the painting which had captured her attention was in truth an original.

'Ah!'

His exclamation endorsed her suspicion, but why should he be regarding her with such a look of furious triumph on his face?

She didn't have long to wait for illumination as he moved swiftly to front her, grabbing her roughly by the shoulders, holding her firmly as if he suspected she was about to take flight.

'So tell me—how is my lovely Lotta? Still as beautiful? Still as acquisitive, hmm?'

'Lotta?' Gina shook her head helplessly. The situation was becoming more bizarre by the minute. 'I don't know any Lotta—my sister's name is Suzie.'

'Suzie. . .' He repeated the name slowly, disbelievingly while his cool regard labelled her a liar.

'You still expect me to believe that your purpose here isn't to steal my Knudsen?'

'You think I'm a thief!' Shock and outrage quelled all other emotions as Gina's eyes flaxed wider in astonishment. She'd never thought her self-imposed assignment would be totally uncomplicated, but this encounter was fast becoming a nightmare!

'What should I think?' His tone was reasonable, his half-smile polite, but his fingers retained their iron hold. 'You come here with some badly rehearsed story. First you are looking for some mystery man called Svend, then it is your sister, but all the time you are taking an inventory of my apartment.'

'I had to look somewhere!' Gina defended herself spiritedly. 'If only to save *you* embarrassment. You were, as you so frankly admitted, hardly dressed for entertaining!'

'That would depend on whom I was expecting to

entertain, and I can assure you I have worn less without feeling embarrassment in the right company.'

'Very likely.' Gina gritted her teeth. 'Then let's say it was I who felt embarrassed!'

'But not too discomfited not to recognise the Knudsen, *vel*?' he returned softly. 'And, before you deny it, let me say I saw your start of recognition. And that puzzles me, because Knudsen has only recently gained critical regard in Denmark. Outside Scandinavia he is virtually unknown. So how come you were so well informed, unless you'd been primed by Lotta in the role of confederate?'

Fire flared in Gina's magnificent grey eyes. She was damned if she would be put through a third degree by this raving lunatic who seemed to have a fixation about someone called Lotta.

'I have no intention of denying anything, nor do I have to explain how I obtained my knowledge to you. . .' Mouth taut, she defied him.

'Only if you really are genuine,' he agreed placidly. 'And you truly do need my help to locate the ephemeral Svend—not to mention your sister.' He paused, brows several shades darker than his hair lifted enquiringly. 'On the other hand, if you've allowed yourself to be persuaded either by Lotta's silver tongue or her golden purse to attempt to defraud me—then your best course of action now would be to make for the door before I remember that the blood of the ancient Vikings still runs in my veins!'

Oh, but how she would have loved to tear herself free from his grasp and storm out of the apartment! Only the knowledge that he might provide some clue in the mystery of Suzie's whereabouts held her prisoner.

'Very well,' she said after a moment's thought, deciding that the only solution was to tell him the truth after all. 'You're quite right. I'd never heard of Knudsen until earlier this morning when I was somewhere over the North Sea on my way from England and I happened to open a magazine aimed at Nordic Airport passengers. Among the articles was one on Knudsen, including several reproductions of his paintings. I found them—compulsive. . .fascinating. . .fantasy and fable mixed, and so beautifully executed, almost photographic in detail, that I couldn't shake their impression from my mind. So when I walked in here and caught sight of the painting on your wall, naturally I responded to its presence!' The free magazine had been one of the perks of British Airways Club Class travel—and one she now regretted having enjoyed!

'Hmm.' His hands left her shoulders as he breathed a sigh of relief, and his gaze locked with hers as if he could read her soul in its depth. 'That I can understand. His work affects me the same way—which is why I bought that painting a few years ago. Since then the art world has begun to acknowledge his genius, and when you consider he's probably about to become one of the most sought-after artists of his generation as his fame spreads outside Scandinavia you will understand my concern when a stranger appears on my doorstep with a curiously inadequate enquiry. It wouldn't be the first time that a man has been seduced by female beauty and been left the poorer for his pleasure, nor the first time Lotta has attempted by stealth to deprive me of something which I value.'

'What a dilemma for you.' Gina gritted her teeth before bestowing her sweetest smile on his stern face. 'Not knowing whether a woman covets your body or your Knudsen!'

'Usually the question wouldn't arise,' he returned smoothly. 'But since Lotta's earlier attempt to snatch it from under my nose by devious means I thought it worthwhile to investigate your credentials a little more thoroughly.'

Gina stared back at him stonily, her mouth still retaining a testimony to that fact. However, it seemed from his more relaxed air that he had accepted she was innocent of being involved in any plot devised by the beautiful and desirable Lotta—whoever she might be! Although she was still awaiting an apology for his high-handed actions.

'I'm sure your method would have been very successful too,' she retorted scathingly. 'If I *had* been involved in petty larceny I certainly wouldn't still be here arguing the point after your abuse!' She glared at him with icy indignation. 'I can assure you I've never had the misfortune to meet your criminally motivated friend, but might I suggest that if you're going to be paranoid about your picture you put it in a bank vault for safety?'

'Certainly not. I bought it to enjoy it.' He frowned reprovingly. 'However, in view of recent events I do intend to get it electronically protected.'

'Which means, since you're declaring your intentions, you've finally decided I'm not a thief?' Gina raised eloquent winged eyebrows, inviting an apology.

'Either that, or I'm pointing out that you've failed on this occasion and will have even less opportunity for success on another.'

'This is the most absurd conversation I've ever had!' Frustration had brought her almost to screaming point. 'Look, all I want to know is if you have a friend called Svend.'

Broad shoulders shrugged beneath the white T-shirt, as he moved away from her. 'Several. Shall we discuss them over a cup of coffee?'

'No—I——Oh, all right, then.' Gina capitulated with as much grace as possible as her companion padded across the room towards another door, beckoning her to follow him. 'I see you still don't trust me alone with the Knudsen,' she commented acidly, as she complied with his instructions.

All she got for her pains was a slight smile but no verbal reply as with efficient ease he filled and switched on a percolator.

Minutes later she was being ushered out of the small but clinically precise kitchenette, and invited to take a seat on one of the chesterfields as he placed a tray containing two bone-china coffee-mugs, milk and sugar on the glass-topped table between them.

Sitting opposite her, he indicated that she should help herself.

'So we have something else in common,' he observed as she declined both milk and sugar, choosing to drink the hot liquid black, as it came.

'You mean as well as Svend?' Leaning forward eagerly, she met his eyes with frank appeal. 'It's really very important——'

'I meant as well as an admiration for the works of Knudsen,' he interrupted softly. 'And don't you think that before we go any further it would be helpful to introduce ourselves?'

'If you think it's necessary.' Gina's dark head dipped in quick agreement. 'My name is Gina Price, and——'

'Rune Christensen.' His firm voice broke into her sentence as he extended a hand to her.

With a small sigh, Gina replaced her mug on the table and reluctantly took the offered handshake. His hand was hard, the skin warm, the pressure firm, as forceful against her own palm as his mouth had been against hers. Irritated by her train of thought, she shook her head impatiently. If only he'd hear her out without interrupting!

'Herre Christensen,' she began again firmly. 'One of

your acquaintances, called Svend, has run off with my sister. Suzie's only seventeen and both I and my mother are frantic about her safety. If they're no longer staying here, perhaps you'll let me know where I can find them. . .'

When it was obvious from the ensuing silence that no information was forthcoming, she demanded accusingly, 'Are you refusing to help me?'

'Not refusing—unable, Frøken Price.' He emphasised the courtesy title, mocking her own use of the formal. Yet how could she call him Rune? What kind of name was that anyway? Wasn't it a kind of stone one cast when telling fortunes? She could do with a glimpse into the future right now, she decided grimly, particularly since it seemed her irritating companion was intent on being obstructive, despite his apparent change of attitude.

'But you said——' she began angrily, her grey eyes stormy.

'That I have several acquaintances called Svend. That is quite true. But none, I assure you, of an age or inclination to elope with an adolescent foreigner! One is a director of *Dem Danske Bank*, another a family doctor, yet another my chief accountant, a fourth is a minister of the Lutheran church, a fifth——'

'All right, all right!' Was it her fault if a good percentage of the Danish nation was called Svend? Used to creating and presenting ideas to a wide variety of clients, she'd grown proud of her capacity to keep her head under pressure, yet from the moment she'd crossed the threshold of this impressive room she'd been put at a distinct disadvantage. Rune Christensen was amusing himself at her expense. A social dilettante with a hang-up about someone called Lotta, and who had nothing better to do than sleep the daylight hours away, she concluded, despising both the man and his attitude! Yet she had to remain civil. He was still her only lead.

His eyes narrowed speculatively at her tart tone. 'Why, I wonder, do you suppose that *I* should know anything of your sister's abductor?'

'Oh!' For a moment she was taken aback, realising for the first time that she hadn't explained herself very well, then, gathering her wits together, she retorted briskly, 'If you hadn't assaulted me and accused me of being a burglar I would have told you that the Svend I'm looking for is a student who met my sister at the Roskilde music festival and afterwards entertained her and her friends here in this apartment for several nights.'

'Here?' Mobile eyebrows lifted. 'That's impossible,' he said flatly. 'For the past four weeks I've been in the Middle East on business, and this place has been empty and locked up.' A quick glance at the steel digital watch on his sinewy wrist and his eyes were washing over her, a hint of malice in their light depths as he dashed her hopes with cruel precision. 'I returned to Copenhagen early this morning and was in the process of catching up on loss of sleep when your serenade on the doorbell awakened me. So it seems that either you are lying as I first suspected, or you've been deliberately misled.'

CHAPTER THREE

'WELL I agree that someone's being misled,' Gina retorted impatiently. 'But why should it be me? You've just said you haven't been around for several weeks. So it's pretty obvious to me that someone else used this apartment in your absence!'

For a few seconds she thought her outburst had fallen on deaf ears, then Rune said softly, 'Yes, of course, you're right. It had temporarily slipped my mind, but someone did have a spare key some while ago. I assumed it had been replaced, but in the circumstances. . .' His brow creased ominously as he pulled his lean length upright. 'Bear with me a moment while I make a phone call.'

Was she getting somewhere at last? Gina sank back on the comfortable couch. From the sudden change in Rune Christensen's demeanour it seemed she might have cause to be optimistic.

'Hanne?' The base of the telephone resembled a flat black rectangular box, the receiver a slender ebony boomerang in Rune's hand as his brisk voice echoed round the room.

The ensuing conversation was unintelligible to Gina but it was very noticeable that her abrasive host never removed his gaze from her expectant face, as if he still harboured doubts about her purpose there, and, if his deepening frown was anything to judge from, the news wasn't going to be good.

'Well?' she demanded, hard pressed to conceal her anxiety as he replaced the receiver on its rest.

'No. It is not well at all!' He made no attempt to

hide his displeasure. 'I've just been speaking to my sister. She tells me that her son has been influenced by some flighty little English madam to renege on his own responsibilities in order to give her a conducted tour of Copenhagen.'

'Your nephew? Svend is your nephew?' Gina made no attempt to disguise her amazement. 'But you told me——'

'That I had many acquaintances named Svend and that none of them would run off with a teenager.' Anger tightened the skin on his high Nordic cheekbones. 'At the time, you remember, you'd given me very little information to go on. As soon as you deigned to tell me that the Svend you were looking for was a student, and that he'd used my home as a hotel, I recalled that my nephew spent a night here shortly after I moved in so that he could attend a lecture at the city university, and that I'd entrusted him with a spare key so he could come and go as he pleased.'

The growled admission obviously gave him no pleasure, and Gina decided it wiser not to point out that in fact he hadn't recalled his generosity until she had prompted his memory!

'A concession he obviously exercised to the full,' she contented herself with murmuring instead, her eyes dancing with amusement as she enjoyed his discomfort, a feeling of relief pervading her that she was about to locate Suzie at last. 'And you have the nerve to call my sister flighty! Tell me—were you just being deliberately perverse with me earlier or had you forgotten you had a nephew called Svend?'

'Svend is hardly an unusual name in Denmark.' He glowered at her. 'Besides, I assumed since you were here in Copenhagen you were seeking a Copenhagener. My nephew lives and studies in Odense on the island of Fyn. Am I supposed to have second sight as to his whereabouts?' His mouth tightened as he discerned the slight turn of her lips. 'You find the matter amusing?'

She let the smile develop to a soft laugh at his expense. 'It seems your concern about security was justified after all. It was just aimed at the wrong person.'

'A circumstance which will be altered when I see Svend again!' His tone was grim. 'He had strict instructions to replace the spare key in its place before he left.'

And, of course, Rune Christensen had never supposed for one moment that his orders would be forgotten or disobeyed! For a fleeting moment Gina almost felt sorry for Hanne's recalcitrant son. There was a mental as well as a physical strength to Svend's uncle and she wouldn't like to be the one who trespassed on his preserves. Viking justice hadn't been renowned for its leniency, she recollected. On the other hand, she comforted herself, the modern Dane, from what she had read and the little she had seen, appeared not to have inherited a great deal from his pillaging ancestors! That Rune Christensen could prove the exception to that rule didn't bear thinking about.

'So where are they staying?' she asked expectantly instead.

'That is precisely what Svend's parents would like to know.' He returned to the couch opposite her, splaying long legs across the almond-green carpet, his bare feet coming within inches of her shoes. 'It seems my nephew is so besotted with your sister that he's treated his parents with arrant discourtesy, walking away from the opportunity of meeting his father's cousin who is flying in from the States—a man who could be influential in his future career. All Hanne knows is that the two of them are staying somewhere in Copenhagen for an indefinite period.' His eyes glittered with an arctic coldness. 'Your sister has a lot to answer for!'

'Suzie has?' Gina sprang to her feet glaring down at the golden-skinned Dane lounging opposite her. 'For heaven's sake! She's only seventeen. It's your nephew who's got all the explaining to do. He's older than she is and probably a lot more experienced. He should know better. How dare he influence her to give up her studies in England to walk the streets of Copenhagen?'

'You're suggesting my nephew is a pimp?'

The silky enquiry brought a flush to Gina's face. She had no doubt that he had deliberately misunderstood her unfortunate phraseology in an attempt to embarrass her.

'How should I know?' she asked boldly. 'If he shares his uncle's hostility towards the female sex he might very well be prepared to treat them with similar contempt!' The stillness of his face should have warned her to stop, but her system was growing warm with the rising level of adrenalin flowing into it. Suzie wasn't without blame in what had happened—that she accepted. Her sister was headstrong and volatile, sometimes thoughtless of the feelings of those who cared for her, but she could also be charming and generous, compassionate and very lovable, and she was certainly no *femme fatale*, to lead a man to his doom against his will. No way was Suzie going to have to answer for Svend's behaviour. In fact the very opposite was true. She looked down her pretty nose at Rune's immobile countenance. 'But if he is he's picked the wrong girl in Suzie. She's not promiscuous!'

'Just a tease—is that what you're saying? That Svend has offended a man who could have been instrumental in his receiving an engineering scholarship to a university in the States, and all he's likely to receive as thanks is a chaste kiss?' He rose slowly to his feet, every movement so controlled that it appeared menacing. Fighting an impulse to back away, Gina forced herself to hold her ground, refusing to let him see how his nearness made the hairs on the back of her neck rise in anticipation of conflict.

'Suzie isn't——' she began belligerently, only to find her voice faltering to a halt as Rune, clearly oblivious to the start of her protest, swept his cool glance over her from the crown of her dark head to the sensible shoes on her graceful feet. She had read of men stripping a woman's clothes away with a look, but it wasn't her apparel that Rune's rapier appraisal discarded. It was her patina of sophistication, the shell that encased her inexperience in dealing with men of Rune Christensen's calibre.

'You're wrong about Svend, *min kaere* Gina Price.' The low timbre of his voice was none the less frightening for all its softness. 'At twenty he is still young and foolish enough to believe that all women are goddesses under the skin. If your sister is as virtuous as you say, then she has nothing to fear from my nephew.' He lifted his hand with graceful ease to imprison her chin, strong fingers splayed against her throat, their touch light but masterful. 'And you're wrong about me too,' he continued evenly. 'I have no hostility towards women in general. In fact they've been instrumental in providing some of the greatest pleasures in my life to date. As for contempt. . .' He paused, holding her entrapped by the power of his presence, as her imagination formed its own pictures of the pleasures her sex had provided for him. 'I reserve that emotion only for people who deserve it.'

'Or those whom you mistakenly suspect of deserving it!' Somewhere she found the spirit to contend his patronising arrogance, although it was impossible to hide the slight quaver in her voice. 'Perhaps you should be more sure of your facts before inflicting punishment for sins committed only in your own imagination!'

'You found my kiss chastening?' he queried gently. Too gently for genuine remorse, because instead of being cut by her rebuke his ego seemed untouched as an inner warmth flooded his face, lighting his eyes as the sun's rays deepened a summer sky. 'Perhaps I have been less civil than you would have reason to expect.' His eyes narrowed on her pale, proud face as she backed away from him, her heart beating so rapidly that it was all she could do not to betray her agitation by raising her hands to calm it.

For the first time she saw small lines of weariness grooving the side of his well-shaped mouth, as his shoulders flexed beneath her gaze. 'If you'd appeared on a day when I wasn't jet-lagged and exasperated by travel delays, I might have reacted less belligerently to your unannounced arrival. I wouldn't want to give the impression that we Danes are anything less than hospitable to our guests—invited or not.'

Rune Christensen falsely penitent was a dangerous animal, Gina realised, smarting from the sting in the tail of his so-called apology, as he'd doubtless intended she should. Even his cynicism couldn't destroy the kind of male magnetism that could draw the innocent female into its web. Only she was no longer innocent, was she? At least not in an emotional sense. Marcus had shattered that soft innocence when he had turned on her like a rabid dog, snapping, destroying, infecting. . . In time she would forget him, but the legacy of sensual awareness he had left her could prove to be a burden more difficult to shed.

'Clearly our ideas of hospitality differ, Herre Christensen,' she retorted, an angry flush touching her cheekbones. 'As does our understanding of the nature of an apology.' She would have stopped there if the

adrenalin in her system had been less potent or the
half-smile on his face hadn't taunted her to further
repartee. 'I wouldn't be surprised if your "lovely
Lotta", whoever she is, *deserves* to have your precious
Knudsen as a reward for having had to put up with
your ideas of chivalry!' Abruptly she turned, determined to leave having had the last word.

'Wait!' She was halfway to the door when Rune's
authoritative command stopped her in her tracks.
'Where do you think you're going?'

'To look for my sister, of course!' Quickly she
reached for the doorknob, only to find her frantic effort
useless as Rune's hand slammed against the door,
holding it fast.

'Where?' If possible his face was even grimmer than
his voice as he barred her exit.

A soupçon of fear mingled with pleasure as Gina
realised that what had meant to have been her parting
shot had touched target. 'Here in Copenhagen, of
course, where, according to you, your wretched
nephew is playing at being a travel courier, instead of
being a dutiful son.'

His laugh was contemptuous. 'You have an intimate
knowledge of the city?'

She bit her lip. 'You know I haven't.'

'On the contrary, I know very little about you at all,
Gina Price. Only that you have a sharp tongue and an
undisciplined sister, neither of which attributes I find
endearing. However, it seems we share a common
purpose—to point out to our rebellious relatives the
grief they are causing their families. In which case,
since Copenhagen isn't the biggest capital in Europe,
the chances are that if we look in the right places we'll
find them sooner or later!'

'We?' Gina echoed faintly.

'Of course.' Amusement veiled the sharpness of the

ice-blue eyes that held her own astonished grey gaze.
'You'll need the help of a Copenhagener, and who
better than I? Not only do I have a personal knowledge
of Svend's appearance but I know all the most likely
places to look.'

'But what about your own work?' she enquired
tentatively, not at all sure she liked the way things were
turning out. The last thing she wanted was to spend
more time with this abrasive Scandinavian.

Wide shoulders shrugged negligently. 'I need a few
hours to report back to the office, then my time can be
my own. Where are you staying?'

She hesitated, unwilling to be railroaded into a
decision. 'I appreciate your offer, but really there's no
need. . .'

'On the contrary, Gina Price. . .' Her name rolled
off his tongue as if it were some rich dessert to be
savoured, and the tiredness seemed suddenly to leave
his face. It was as if the dominance of his spirit had
conquered the physical results of lack of sleep, lending
him a new vitality which arced across the distance
between them, charging her own weakened batteries,
as he responded to a challenge which had been originally hers. 'I insist—for Hanne's sake.'

Silence hung heavily between them as Gina hesitated, torn between her own instinctive need to put as
much distance between herself and this overpowering
Norseman as possible, and her fear of not acting in
Suzie's best interests.

'Well?' He read her indecision. 'If you're really as
concerned about Suzie as you pretend. . .'

Pretend! The word flailed her as he must surely have
intended. Hadn't she already taken time off work
which she could ill afford in her sister's interests? Was
the further sacrifice of having to spend more time with

this Danish dictator, this Nordic Nero, really too much for her to endure?

Amused by her own alliterative descriptions, she smiled, only to pull her mouth into stern control as she saw the resulting flash of triumph which illuminated Rune's features.

'Fine.' To her chagrin he took her acceptance for granted. 'Where are you staying?'

Wordlessly Gina reached into a pocket and produced the hotel's business card.

'Yes, I know it.' His glance was perfunctory. 'I'll meet you in the foyer at seven o'clock this evening, and we'll find somewhere to eat first. Then we'll take a tour of the jazz clubs. Since music appears to be the common interest which brought them together, that would seem a logical place to start.'

A spark of antagonism flickered in Gina's eyes, quickly subdued as Rune made a sudden movement, causing her to strain away from his body in a reflex action. But, as he reached across her to open the door and her fear of being touched didn't materialise, her heartbeat steadied and, contenting herself with a curt nod, she stepped across the threshold and walked briskly down the passageway and out of his sight.

Wow! That had been some encounter! she admitted as, regaining the sanctuary of the street, she drew in a deep breath of refreshing air before turning into the road which she remembered from her map-reading would lead her into a series of narrow streets closed to traffic, and known familiarly to the local inhabitants as Strøget.

Stretching a mile from the Rådhuspladsen to Kongens Nytorv, Copenhagen's largest square, the complex enjoyed the fame of being Europe's longest traffic-free shopping precinct. A shiver of anticipation thrilled through her. Suzie loved window-shopping, so wasn't there a possibility that she might be here, that her quest could end in the next hour or so and she would be spared the ordeal of seeing Rune Christensen again?

Slackening her step, she felt hope renewing itself as she strolled along the pavements past tubs of flowering plants interspersed with benches crowded with people resting their tired feet or simply sitting back and enjoying the sunshine while they watched the passers-by. Every variety of shop was there, tempting her to stop. Mainly she resisted the urge in case Suzie should slip past unnoticed, although once or twice she was drawn to pause at some unusual display, particularly of traditional Danish knitwear or shops specialising in the typical and beautiful amber jewellery for which the country was famed.

Now and again the walkway became even more narrow as a pavement café spilled its chairs and tables upon it, tempting the strolling shopper to stop for refreshment; here and there a small crowd gathered around a solitary musician or a group of young teenagers singing, the plates at their feet covered in *kroner* as a testament to their audience's approval.

Every so often she caught a glimpse of the green, tiered wedding-cake-style steeple of St Nikolai church rising two hundred and thirty feet into the air. Once she allowed herself to stray away from the main concourse, lured by the strains of a string quartet, to find herself in a large square dominated by a giant plane tree. People thronged in the several outdoor cafés, while others sat in groups on the paving stones, enjoying the music, cans of Coke at their feet, slices of *smørrebrød* in their hands, while neatly stacked against the railings of the old houses with their terracotta- and gamboge-painted façades were the ubiquitous bicycles which were so much a part of the Danish travel scene.

But as the hours passed her optimism waned. It

seemed she was not to be rid of Svend's dictatorial uncle so easily. In which case she might just as well be punctual for their mutually unwelcome assignation, rather than give him cause for further sarcasm at her expense!

Threading her way as diligently as she could through the mass of humanity, it was with a sigh of relief that she eventually found herself back in the vast City Hall square. From there a brisk fifteen-minute walk would take her back to her hotel.

Half an hour later, dressed only in her favourite ecru-coloured bodyshaper, she grimaced as she surveyed the contents of the wardrobe. From what she had observed during the afternoon, 'casual' was the order of the day.

Oh, well, it would have to be the linen dress. At least it was well cut, as befitted the Harvey Nichols label inside it, and the muted fuchsia shade flattered her pale skin; she would wear her softly quilted black waterproof jacket over it as a concession to the cooler northern nights. As for her hair. . .perhaps something more sophisticated? Earlier in the day she'd allowed Rune to get beneath her skin, disturb her customary veneer of being in control. Now was her chance to let him see the image of herself that everyone else saw. Cool, suave, sophisticated—in control of her own life.

Her mouth tight with resolution, she returned her attention to her hair. Thick, dark and naturally wavy as it was, all she had to do was twist it through an elasticated hairband and pin the resulting pony-tail into whatever shape pleased her at the moment. This evening a figure eight would do, reaching from crown to nape.

Satisfied with the merest hint of make-up she had used on her heart-shaped face, she emptied out the small jewellery sachet she always took with her on her travels. Fun earrings were her indulgence. Tonight she would wear the swinging strands of rolled gold ending in one large crystal drop. Well, that was it. Finally she stepped into her chosen dress, zipping it up at the back with practised ease. She'd made the deadline with minutes to spare. A final spray of expensive perfume and she was leaving the room.

Rune was waiting for her in the foyer as she stepped out of the lift. It was only then, when her heart leaped alarmingly and her pulse quickened in immediate response, that she realised she'd been half expecting he wouldn't keep the date. At least, she decided approvingly, dressed now in sharply creased fawn trousers and dark brown casual shirt in fine wool beneath a soft leather jacket, he appeared less of the savage she'd encountered earlier in the day! Hopefully the evening wouldn't turn out to be the disaster she'd envisaged.

'I congratulate you on your punctuality.' His light eyes swept in quick appraisal from her new hairstyle to the sandals which graced her nyloned feet, before he opened the door leading to the patio, standing back so she could precede him.

'I wouldn't have dared to be late,' she flung back over her shoulder, hoping he recognised the sarcasm in her tone.

'Very wise.' As he fell into step beside her he took her arm, gently guiding her as they turned into the main street. 'When we Danes give and accept terms in an agreement we expect to keep them—and see them kept!'

CHAPTER FOUR

'THIS is a waste of time!' Despair lent a soft vulnerability to Gina's countenance as she searched yet another dimly lit room with troubled eyes. Five different venues in less than five hours and they'd drawn a blank at all of them!

'You disappoint me. I thought it was time very well spent.' Across the small table in the basement club where they now sat, Rune's light eyes challenged her statement. 'Are you saying you didn't enjoy your meal after all?'

'No, I'm not saying that!' An odd tremor of expectation thrilled through her as she held his slightly mocking glance. The evening had commenced at a restaurant where Rune had introduced her to *koldt bord*, the pan-Scandinavian cold buffet-style spread, while he'd taken the opportunity of finding out more details about Suzie, including her appearance. Although she'd helped herself only sparingly from the selection ranging from herring in various preparations through varieties of other seafood to choices of pâtés and cuts of prime meat accompanied by several types of bread and salads, she'd found the meal delicious and satisfying.

'Then it's the jazz clubs that displease you?' His look of innocent enquiry was infuriating.

'You know exactly what I mean,' she reproved, too aware that her pleasure in the music had been mirrored on her face more than once during their tour of the nightspots to be able to disavow her delight in the entertainment. 'It's two o'clock in the morning and we're nowhere nearer to finding Suzie.'

'On the contrary.' Rune's mouth twisted wryly. 'We've achieved a great deal. I've spoken to several of the barmen, explaining our dilemma, and elicited a promise that if a couple answering to the description of Svend and your sister put in an appearance and are conversing in English the man shall be discreetly asked if he is Svend Eriksen and, if so, requested to get in touch with me. Although their detection might have been easier had you thought to bring a photograph of your sister with you,' he rebuked her softly.

Privately Gina agreed with him. It had been a stupid omission, but then she'd left so unexpectedly and in such a rush; besides, she'd expected Suzie to be at the address she'd been given.

'As I've already told you, we're very alike, except that Suzie's hair is very short and curly and, of course, she's much younger,' she retorted with some spirit. 'I could say the same thing to you about a photograph of Svend!'

'Oddly enough, such an item doesn't have priority in my wallet,' he murmured condescendingly. 'Had I had any idea what I was coming home to, I should have assured in advance that such a likeness would be instantly available.'

Ignoring the edge of sarcasm audible in his reply, and making no attempt to conceal her scepticism, she asked instead, 'You really believe Svend will get in touch with you if he receives the message?'

'*Ja*, I think so. He is not totally without conscience,' he returned complacently.

'Then he must have switched it off when he persuaded Suzie not to return to England with her friends as planned.' Gina glared across the table at him, uncomfortably aware that he was the source of her unreasonable impatience, and resentful of the effect his presence was having on her.

His eyes narrowed speculatively. 'Why is it, I wonder, that you always see your sister as being blameless? Can it be that you have no idea of the power a young, nubile girl can exercise over a young, impressionable male?'

'Because I know her—besides, she's still at school!' Gina returned quickly.

Rune gave a short, mirthless laugh. 'Since when has a metaphorical gym-slip been a deterrent when a beautiful adolescent sets her sights on a young and virile man?'

'That's a disgusting thing to say. You make my sister sound like some predatory Lolita! And what makes you think Suzie is beautiful? I didn't say that.'

'No, but you said she was like you.' He met her cool stare, examining the liquid softness of her pupils intently. 'And you, *min skat*, are very beautiful, as I'm sure you are fully aware.'

Try as she might, Gina couldn't stop the blush that rose to her cheeks at his unwanted and unexpected compliment. In the pre-Marcus days she'd seemed to have greater control over every aspect of her nervous system than she did now. Grateful for the low lights, she gritted her teeth, hopeful that her companion wouldn't be aware of her reaction.

All evening she'd been aware of him not only as the uncle of the delinquent who had abducted Suzie, but also on a separate level she had no wish to analyse. Now the slow burn of his steady gaze awakened feelings within her which were scary. Neither was she too happy about the epithet '*min skat*', which he'd applied to her for the second time that day. It reminded her too much of the English word 'scatty', and she was neither feather-brained nor flighty! If that was the impression she was giving, then the fault lay entirely with him for disturbing her usual equilibrium with his unexpected behaviour.

'Of course I appreciate your giving up your time on my behalf,' she began stiffly, 'but——'

'Good.' His blond head dipped briefly, as he refused her the possibility of completing what he must have guessed would have been a remonstrative retort. 'Although, for the record, I'm acting on Hanne's behalf as much as yours. She and her husband Jens have worked hard to give their three children a good start in life. We live in an increasingly competitive world where good qualifications are a passport to success. Svend was doing very well at college. He's a bright young man who, until he fell into your sister's clutches, was very keen on meeting his father's cousin to discuss a possible scholarship in the States. Unfortunately, Jens and Hanne are dairy farmers and cannot spend time away from their stock to find him and try to make him see sense.'

'You mean if he doesn't show up at the right time the opportunity won't occur again?' The tone of her voice echoed her disbelief.

'I mean that we still follow the old custom of behaving courteously to our family and friends. For Svend not to keep the appointment he made, solely to pleasure himself with the attractions of Copenhagen, will be regarded as an act of arrant rudeness, and will almost certainly disqualify him from gaining the approval of my brother-in-law's cousin who himself is an ex-patriate Dane.' His eyes held hers with a thoughtful appraisal. 'How about you, Gina? Is your mother perhaps a widow or divorcee, or do you have a father who is too busy to exert authority over his wayward daughter? Is that why the job has been deputed to you?'

'My father knows nothing about Suzie's escapade,' she returned quickly. 'He—he's a professional golfer, you see. Oh, not in the top flight, but he travels around the world—anywhere golf is played. It's difficult to contact him, because he's always on the move.' Her voice trailed away in despair as she considered just how poor a husband and father Campion Price had been to his family.

'But he would be worried about his youngest daughter if he did know, *nej*?' Rune frowned as his eagle-eyed regard read the despair on her face.

'Of course!' Gina's confirmation came just a little too fast, as family pride forced the lie to her lips. Campion Price had wanted sons. Boys who would turn into men and follow him round the world, stand beside him at bars, exchange vulgarities, share the favours of the golf groupies, the young girls and some not so young, who hung around any group of sportsmen. Campion Price had never cared for the emotional welfare of his wife—let alone his daughters!

She choked down the sudden lump in her throat, rejecting a surge of self-pity she had no need for. So, her childhood had been spent in boarding schools—so what? Hadn't she finally made it as an integrated human being without the help of her father?

'And your mother?' he persisted. 'She didn't consider accompanying you on the search for her daughter?'

'No.' She owed this irritating man no explanation—yet out of fairness to Margaret, whose concern was painfully felt, she felt obliged to qualify her first short answer. 'My mother felt that Suzie would be more inclined to listen to me because there had been a certain amount of friction between the two of them recently.'

'I see. And it was simple for you to take a holiday?'

Again the keen eyes dwelt perceptively on her strained face. 'You had no jealous lover, no demanding boss to make your absence difficult?'

'I could be married—a housewife—a lady of leisure. . .' she began, irritated by his questions.

'Ah, but you're not.' He seized her left hand across the table. 'Not only do you not wear a wedding-ring, but you have the air, the aura of sexual uncertainty which belies a history of nights spent in connubial bliss.' He smiled gently as she tore her hand from his grasp. 'So tell me, Gina Price, what do you do for a living?'

There was no reason why she should satisfy his curiosity and she was honest enough to admit that the only reason for doing so was because she was proud of her success. 'I'm a copywriter at Grantham and Marsh—a top London advertising agency,' she responded coolly, finding it unnecessary to add that, because of the recession at present affecting the advertising world generally, her job might not be waiting for her on her return! Let him see her as the successful career-woman she was. Sexual uncertainty indeed! How dared he make such judgements on such a brief acquaintance—and how mortifying that he was right about her inadequacies.

'And since we're exchanging personal details, Rune Christensen,' she countered briskly, 'what about you? How come you are so easily spared from the company which employs you?'

'Hmm. . .' He pursed his lips thoughtfully and the hidden laughter in his eyes warned her that she might not like his answer. 'Possibly because the new ventilation system I've recently supervised being installed in a factory in one of the Arab Emirates has proved so successful that I have orders for two more, or possibly because I've just spent four weeks at full stretch in a very hot country with very little relaxation and deserve a holiday—but more probably because I own a majority stockholding in the company I bought cheap and built up to its present eminence, which gives me the position of chairman and managing director and full autonomy in deciding what I do, where I do it and with whom.'

'Bully for you!' She flashed him a false smile of congratulation. 'And how fortunate you have no female—er—encumbrances to consider before making your dynamic decisions.' She arched her eyebrows enquiringly, smiling into his watchful face, her pulse beating a little faster as some wicked impulse prompted her to bait him. 'Or,' she added with deliberate coquetry, 'am I mistaken in assuming that the light-fingered Lotta is no longer a part of your—er—personal life?'

Had she gone too far? The sudden tenseness of his jaw suggested that discretion would have been the better part of valour, and so it should have been, if he hadn't taunted her about her sexual uncertainty. Stoically she continued to meet his gaze with an expression of polite interest carefully assumed to disguise the way her heart had increased its beating.

His eyes bored into hers like gimlets, cool and beautiful and unforgiving. 'You may assume whatever makes you happy about my—er—personal life, *min søde* Gina.' Mockingly he copied her own deliberate hesitancy, before pushing his chair back and rising to his feet. 'And now I think the time has come to explore a little further.' He lifted her jacket from the back of her chair, inviting her to wear it.

'Another club? Doesn't anything ever close in Copenhagen?' Obediently she slid her arms inside the coat, suppressing a yawn, recoiling instantly as she felt the firm touch of his hands brush her shoulders.

What on earth was the matter with her? She'd only

known him a few hours yet every cell of her body seemed sensitised to his presence. It was a disturbing and unpleasant sensation. She'd always thought that the phrase 'going weak at the knees' was an over-used cliché with no reference to reality, yet that was exactly how she felt. As if she were being asked to walk across a sheet of ice, and with every step her confidence was faltering. The end result of such a venture, she reminded herself sharply, was inevitably a fall!

'I'm sorry, what did you say?' Sternly she dragged her thoughts and reactions under control, as Rune guided her through the crowded room towards the exit.

'Just that Copenhagen likes to be known as the city that never sleeps,' he repeated easily. 'Things get a little quiet between five and seven in the morning, but even then there are places open if you know where to look. It's possible to spend the entire night enjoying oneself and ending up having a good Copenhagen breakfast of meat and cheese, yoghurt and *wienerbrød*. . .'

'*Wienerbrød*?' She picked up the unfamiliar word, relieved to be discussing impersonal things once more.

'Ah, a direct translation would be Viennese bread, but in England I believe you call them Danish pastries—an amusing quirk of language, *ja*?'

'*Ja*,' Gina acknowledged faintly as they emerged into the street. 'I hope you're not planning anything like that tonight!'

'Not if you don't feel up to it.' There was no tiredness perceptible on Rune's blandly enquiring face as he shrugged his wide shoulders into his own jacket. Presumably he had snatched a few more hours' sleep, she decided morosely, while she'd been traipsing fruitlessly up and down Strøget.

'Is it really worth going somewhere else?' she asked a trifly wistfully, filling her lungs with cool fresh air and realising for the first time that the pavements were damp and it must have been raining.

'Trust me. It's not far and it will be the last place tonight. It doesn't start to fill up until late, but it's very popular, especially with the younger crowd.' Rune brushed aside her lack of enthusiasm with such purpose that she had no option but to fall into step beside him.

Ib's Club was similar to the others she'd visited, but more so, Gina decided a few minutes later as wearily she followed Rune into its depths: deeper, darker, more packed, the music more rawly evocative. It seemed like a minor miracle when she found herself seated within touching distance of the small group of musicians, until she realised that Rune was well-known here, not only by the management but, as the current number drew to a triumphant close, to the players as well, as they drew him on to the low rostrum and surrounded him with much back-slapping and laughter.

'They've promised to keep an eye out for our miscreants,' he told her, returning to the tiny table. 'Unfortunately they're demanding payment for their services.'

'Well, that's all right!' She wasn't wealthy, but a small reward wouldn't break her. 'If they can locate Suzie I'll willingly pay them.'

'Sorry, but I'm the one being held to ransom.' He pulled off his jacket, throwing it casually across the back of his chair. 'I've told them I'll pay, but not before I'm ready!'

'But. . .' she started to protest, but he was already walking away from her, weaving his way through the seated audience, shouldering past the standing groups. Minutes later he came back into view, a bottle in one hand, two tiny glasses in the other.

'Aquavit,' he explained tersely. 'Guaranteed to put new life into you.'

'You've bought a whole bottle?' Gina's voice rose in astonishment. She hadn't needed to speak Danish to realise the contents of the bottle: the water of life. . . call it would you would. . .it was pure unadulterated spirit and it had its equivalent in every country of the world which indulged in alcohol, so potent it should only be consumed in small doses as the tiny, liqueur-sized vessels that Rune placed on the table testified. . .

'Relax, *min skat*.' There was cool laughter in his eyes. 'You are not being led into a drunken orgy. Be assured the barman knows exactly how much liquid there is in this bottle. We drink what we wish and when we return the bottle to him we will be charged accordingly.'

Before she could protest, he had filled both glasses. For a moment she hesitated, then gave a mental shrug. Apart from a glass of lager at dinner she had been drinking only fruit juices, while Rune's own consumption of lager had been only moderate, not enough to have much effect on a man of such highly tuned physique, she comforted herself. A taste of aquavit would do her no harm.

She lifted her glass, only to have her arm stilled.

'Wait, there is something else I must teach you. In Denmark it is usual to toast one's friends before drinking.'

'Oh, yes, of course,' she nodded. 'I know what you mean—it's like clinking glasses in England and saying "cheers".'

'No, it is not!' His hold on her arm tightened, preventing her from turning her words into actions. '*Kom*, I will show you. First you hold your glass towards me—and I mine towards you.'

He released his grasp, allowing her to follow his example.

'Next, we look into each other's eyes, like this.'

There it was again: that feeling of being mesmerised as obediently she met the ice-blue gaze which devoured her. How could such overt coolness evoke the wave of such intense heat which flooded through every cell of her body? Why should her pulse-beat grow light and fast and her mouth become so dry that the impulse to lick her lips was mandatory? Her hand trembled but she couldn't even tear her gaze away to check whether any of the liquid had spilt, as Rune's low, intense voice continued smoothly. 'Then we say "*skål*" and drink, and the way we drink aquavit is like this—all at once!'

He broke eye-contact, lifting his glass to his mouth, throwing his head back and tossing down the contents of the glass with one smooth action.

Blindly, Gina followed suit, gasping as the spirit hit her throat like a million splinters of ice, freezing first then burning, bringing tears to her eyes.

'And then,' Rune continued inexorably, 'you must hold out your glass towards me once more and again meet my eyes. This way a man may always read who is his friend and who his enemy.'

Gina obeyed, wishing she could avoid that piercing appraisal, feeling as trapped as a hypnotist's victim. Angry—because wasn't it accepted that an individual could only be influenced if she was a willing party? But only once in her life had she willingly allowed a man to break through her protective barriers, and the pain still smarted. She wondered if she had developed an early warning system since the fiasco with Marcus. Perhaps that was why every cell of her normally controlled body seemed to be on red alert in Rune Christensen's presence.

How long she would have stared into his beautiful cool eyes before he chose to release her she'd never know, because at that moment the band struck into the opening bars of 'If you knew Suzie', demanding her attention as with an exclamation of pleased surprise she half turned to watch them, her mouth curling into a spontaneous smile.

'Gina. . .' Rune spoke her name thoughtfully, his deep tone audible beneath the surge of brass and drums. 'An interesting name. . . That sounds more Italian than English to me.'

'My maternal grandfather was Italian,' she surprised herself by replying, reaching for her refilled glass, extending it towards Rune and going once more through the motions he had taught her. '*Skål!*'

Look, drink, look again. . .this time it was easy because *she* had instigated the toast. She commanded Rune's gaze briefly and dismissed it with disdain. Now, why had she told him that? The fact that Margaret had been illegitimate, a war baby conceived between an Italian prisoner of war and an English landgirl, had no bearing on her name, although probably quite a lot to do with Margaret's lack of maternalism, since she'd been reared in a children's home. It had been Campion Price, her father, who, disappointed that his firstborn had not been the male he'd intended naming after his own father, had insisted she bore the feminine version of that name—Georgina.

She gasped as the liquid hit her tonsils, waiting for them to unfreeze, swallowing with difficulty but no pain.

'But actually I was christened Georgina,' she volunteered in a hoarse whisper, when she could speak again. 'Oh, dear lord, what's happened to my vocal cords?' One slender hand rose to her throat as her grey eyes widened in alarm.

'Temporary anaesthesia, that's all.'

As Rune laughed at her discomfort she was filled with a sudden urge to fling herself at him: wipe the laughter from his face, annihilate the sudden disarming dimples which had appeared beneath his lean cheeks, seal his mouth so that the corners couldn't turn so distractingly upwards at her expense. Stunned by the images of her own mind, all she could do was clench and unclench her fists, praying the numbing effect she had encouraged would disapper as quickly as Rune had implied.

He leaned towards her, his voice pitched confidentially low. 'In Denmark we say that aquavit is strong as a Viking, fiery as a lover, cold as an iceberg and fresh as a virgin. An interesting thought, *nej*?' He reached across and took her own unresisting hand in his own, lacing his fingers through hers. 'Together you and I could generate the power of aquavit, I believe. For me the strength and passion—for you the ice and freshness, *ja*?'

Wordlessly Gina met his gaze. Cold, yes. Unattainable, yes. That was the impression she had always wanted to give. But she had wanted to give it from a position of power, of strength. She wanted men to believe that she was choosy, not that she had never chosen. That was the only way she could exist with men in a man's world. Was it possible that this percipient Norseman had recognised that she was still unviolated? Did she wear her virginity like a name-badge at a conference? Her breath sawed painfully in her throat. She had always believed there would be someone special—for a while she had been under the illusion that that someone was Marcus. She had found out painfully and publicly that she had been mistaken.

It was ridiculous to be ashamed of her lack of experience, to feel only half a woman, to envy Suzie her ability to give herself mentally and emotionally and doubtless physically without thought or recrimination. She herself had long ceased to believe in Father Christmas and fairy-tales. Wasn't it time she stopped believing in love since she had no evidence to suggest that such an unselfish, uplifting emotion existed outside the imagination of those who wanted to be duped? She shivered, running her hands along her bare arms, feeling the goose-pimples.

'There is no you and I,' she denied the hypothesis vehemently. 'Nor could there ever be!'

'You don't believe in fairy-tales, then?' He leaned towards her, uncannily reading her mind, sleek eyebrows lifted in gentle interrogation.

'Of course not!' Hastily she denied any such sentimentality. 'Does anyone?'

'Hans Christian Andersen?' he suggested softly. 'He once said, "Every man's life is a fairy-tale written by God's fingers." Perhaps you should relax a little, and—who knows—perhaps you'll find your own happy ending where you least expect it, and now, if you'll excuse me, the time has come to reward my friends in advance for the efforts they have promised to make on our behalf.'

CHAPTER FIVE

PUSHING back his chair, Rune rose to his feet, flexing his shoulder muscles before mounting the rostrum.

Astonishment rounding her eyes, Gina watched as one of the band handed him a trumpet. There was a brief discussion before another member of the group stepped forward and made an announcement, the only words making any sense to her being those of Rune's name. With a sinking heart she waited for what was about to come. Was Rune about to make a fool of himself? Was this to be the price of winning his friends' help?

The next moment the music started, sending a thrill of expectation lancing through her as she instantly recognised the opening bars of 'Sweet Georgia Brown'. Was it her imagination or had the crowd surrounding her gone unusually quiet as Rune lifted the instrument to his lips? As the notes rose clear and true, all anxiety on his behalf left her. Rune was a competent player—more than that, he was good! It was a melody she had always loved; now, in this packed cellar, played by this golden-skinned Dane who both intrigued and irritated her, it took on an even deeper significance, melting her bones, flowing through her, drawing her senses towards the man who had been yesterday's stranger.

As the final notes quivered into silence and he left the stage to tumultuous applause, she rose to her feet in spontaneous acclaim for his effort. 'I used to belong to one of the university jazz bands when I was studying here in Copenhagen,' he told her easily. 'I just play for relaxation nowadays, but I know two of the guys who play here regularly and from time to time they invite me to join them.'

'You're excellent!' Gina gave him the unstinted praise he deserved.

'It must be in my blood.' He waved aside her admiration. 'The Danes have always been handy at blowing horns. You must have noticed the *lur* blowers' statue in the Rådhuspladsen?' He slanted her a speculative glance.

'The two Viking warriors, you mean?' she nodded. 'Very imposing, but not as fascinating as the fountain with the bull and dragon fighting.'

'Ah, there you would be wrong, *min skat*. The *lur* blowers are far more intriguing because local legend has it that every time a virgin walks past them the sound of the *lur* echoes round the square.' He shrugged his shoulders. 'Of course, no one knows if the legend is true because. . .' He left the sentence unfinished, reaching for her as she would have retaken her seat, drawing her into his arms before she had realised his intention. 'Not so fast, sweet Georgina Price. I think I deserve a small gesture of gratitude for my effort, don't you?'

It sounded like a question, but he had never intended to wait for her answer. Even as she tried to evade him, he was drawing her closer, making the blood sing in her veins as he smiled down at her, the hypnotic blue eyes half shuttered but still as powerful, as he raised a firm hand to the back of her head, guiding her face towards his own, his mouth seeking the trembling softness of hers, hard and demanding as it reached its goal, yet instantly becoming as gentle and manipulative as it had been when he had coaxed the throbbing melody from the borrowed trumpet.

But she wasn't made of brass, or ice either, although she tried to close her mind to what he was doing, to the gentle, unbearable pleasure of his lips moving slowly over hers, not cruel as they had been earlier, but coaxing, first lightly and then more demanding. A tidal wave of desire powered through her—breathtaking and terrifying, a craving so fierce that she surrendered completely to the sweet persistence of his seductive mouth. When his free hand tightened against the small of her back, she made no effort to resist it, glorifying in the feel of his rock-hard body against her own yielding flesh.

She was high on music and aquavit. . .her natural caution smothered by events outside her control. . . Vainly some remaining logical part of her mind sought excuses but was drowned by the sheer surge of basic responses she'd never known she possessed. No magician could have caused her heart to thunder as it was against Rune's own, no mesmerist provoked the answering fire she felt as Rune's kiss became more urgent.

Gradually he had drawn her slightly away from their table, backing her against a shadowed wall. In the background she could hear the band performing another number, the muted hum of conversation as people went about their own business and then, sharply, intrusively, a voice almost in her ear. Musically pitched, intimate, amused—a woman's voice, addressing Rune in Danish.

He was slow to release her, holding her even when his mouth had disclaimed hers, turning his golden head slowly to greet the newcomer, one arm still possessively around her waist.

The woman was beautiful, her delicately fine face capped with shining ash-blonde hair, her blue eyes enhanced by a flutter of dark lashes. The turquoise dress she wore was of the kind of stretch cotton which showed up any figure fault and which in this instance merely demonstrated the perfection of her body.

Flushed and embarrassed, Gina stood in the unwelcome shelter of Rune's implacable arm, feeling both cheap and gauche before such studied perfection, while he calmly continued to converse. Irrational anger tautened her spine. How dare he look so composed, so unaffected by what had just happened between them, when her own stomach felt as if it were the epicentre of an earthquake?

It was only when the other girl paused in the middle of saying something and turned an enquiring face in her own direction, eyebrows raised enquiringly, a patronising smile on her flawless countenance, that Rune appeared to recollect her existence!

'Gina—I'd like you to meet Lotta Petterson—Lotta, this is Gina Price, a friend of mine from England.' He made the simple introduction with formal precision.

Gina smiled weakly. Somehow she'd already guessed the other woman's identity. Trust Rune Christensen to have been involved with the most exquisite-looking woman in the room!

'Ah—so Rune is showing you the sights of Copenhagen, is he?' Lotta acknowledged the introduction with a slight nod of her splendid head. 'I expect you find it very provincial after London—boring, *nej*? Myself, I come from Stockholm.' Denying Gina the opportunity of making the quick contradiction which sprang to her lips, she addressed herself to Rune in her excellent, slightly accented English.

'Darling—how about a toast to new friends and old lovers?' Two quick steps took her to the vacated table where she seized the bottle of aquavit, neatly topping up both glasses. Retaining one for herself, she handed the other to Gina. 'Get another glass for yourself, *min søde*, will you?' The smile she flashed into Rune's brooding face was so blinding that he must have wished he'd brought sunglasses with him, Gina thought uncharitably, wondering how he would take his peremptory dismissal to the bar.

For one moment he hesitated, provoking her to give in to the gentle malice which settled inside her. It was an impossible situation for her—caught between these two beautiful protagonists, whose shared glances spoke louder than their tongues and in a language she had no difficulty in understanding!

'Yes, run along, Rune,' she ordered sweetly. 'Don't keep us waiting!'

A narrow smile thinned his lips but the look he cast on her was scalpel-sharp before he turned in unexpected obedience.

'Congratulations!' Lotta ushered Gina back to the table, seating herself in Rune's chair and indicating Gina should join her. 'Rune is a splendid lover, *ja*? A little mean with his possessions, a little dull in the boardroom—but exciting in the bedroom!' She laughed delightedly, whether at her own linguistic skill or happy memories of Rune's electrifying performances beneath the duvet, Gina didn't know and didn't want to find out!

'I think you're mistaken,' she said frostily. 'Mr Christensen and I aren't——'

'Oh, there's no need to feel bad about it! I've never asked him to be faithful to me. Unfortunately he's reactionary enough not to accord me the same freedom!' Her smile became confidential. 'You know what men are like—swearing that their casual lovers are of no account, yet going berserk when we tell them the same thing!' She sighed. 'This isn't the first time in the past two years he's stalked out of our house in a jealous rage, swearing that this time our relationship is over for good.'

Her beautifully made-up eyes lingered appraisingly on Gina's face before drifting down her body then returning. 'I must say I admire his choice on this occasion; you really are quite attractive. Most of the women he goes off with when we have a bad row are certainly not the type which would make me jealous—which, of course, is the main purpose of the exercise! Why else would he bring you here on his first night back in Denmark when he knows it's one of my favourite clubs?' She gave a low, attractive laugh. 'Of course the whole thing is ridiculous. All our friends know he's infatuated with me and always comes back when his temper has cooled down. Last time it happened he actually asked me to marry him! Can you imagine that?'

She held up her glass of spirit, checking its clarity against the available light. 'Do you know, I'm coming to the conclusion that the time is fast approaching when I may accept his proposal? After all, he's quite a handsome guy in his own way, isn't he, as well as being disgustingly wealthy, and after two years love-games can become depressingly boring, can't they?'

'Two excellent reasons for marriage,' Gina agreed, determined not to show her antipathy towards both Lotta and her philosophy. Damn Rune for kissing her in public and making her vulnerable to this barely disguised attack. Because that was what it was. Beneath Lotta's overt air of comradeship, her claws and teeth were clearly visible.

She cast a quick look towards the bar; praying that Rune would soon return and save her from his mischievous lover. The last thing she wanted was to be a pawn between the two of them, and wasn't that just what Rune had made her by drawing deliberate attention to himself on the stage before making an exhibition of both of them?

'I'm so glad you understand.' It was almost a purr as Lotta's eyes blazed a totally false smile at her. 'Since you're a visitor here, I wouldn't want you to be hurt by Rune's thoughtlessness. I'm afraid some of the other women he played around with when we were having one of our squalls didn't understand the situation. They really believed he cared for them. You see, Rune's the kind of man who will stop at nothing to get and keep what he wants.'

'Like the Knudsen?' Gina asked silkily, provoked beyond politeness.

'He told you about that?' For the first time Lotta appeared taken aback, before rallying. 'I suppose he made me out to be some kind of thief! Don't be alarmed. It's all part of the games we play to make our reunion, when it comes, more blissful. Rune knows it's a bit of fun. He just pretends to believe I'm really after it to add to the stimulation of the game!'

Just as he'd gone out of his way to bait Lotta by kissing her, Gina, so passionately! Gina gritted her teeth in an attempt to keep her temper under control. How dared Rune set her up like this? Determined to let Rune's volatile lover know the truth—that, far from being lovers themselves, she and Rune were nothing more than strangers linked by a common family crisis—she began firmly, 'Look, Lotta—there's something you should know. Rune and I. . .'

But before she could finish the sentence she felt a hand on her shoulder and turned to find Rune looming over her, glass in hand.

'Please don't pour another one. Have mine.' She stood up, offering him her own small full glass. 'I've had more than enough for tonight.' In more ways than one, she could have added but refrained from doing so with an effort.

'Gina is anxious to return to bed, I think,' Lotta taunted smilingly, lifting her glass towards him. '*Skål!*'

'*Skål!*' Rune emptied his glass down his throat in one swift swallow, the pantomime of the toast completely ignored. 'Since I, too, find the prospect of a good night's rest attractive, I must ask you to excuse us.'

He bowed slightly from the waist, an elegant formal gesture more Teutonic than Danish, before taking Gina firmly by one hand, the bottle of aquavit in the other, and marching her towards the bar.

'I hope you're satisfied!' She waited until they were once more outside on the pavement before rounding on him. 'That was just about the most disgusting exhibition I've ever been subjected to!'

'But you said you enjoyed it. . .'

'You know what I mean!' His look of innocence inflamed her already barely held temper. 'I'm not talking about your performance on the trumpet. Why didn't you tell Lotta that our relationship is purely business instead of encouraging her to believe that we were—were——?'

'Sleeping together?' He shrugged broad shoulders, not even going through the motions of denying her accusation. 'Perhaps I wanted to convince her that I had found a replacement for her and she was wasting her time in trying to fan burned-out ashes to life.'

'Or perhaps you were using me to make her jealous?' she suggested tartly.

'If that's what you prefer to believe,' he returned coolly, his face expressionless.

'Then let me tell you that you have no right to include me in your sordid games. I've had just about enough trouble from you and your family.' She was trembling with anger and tiredness, her legs a little unsteady from the effect of the aquavit, as she realised that it had begun to rain again. 'Is it possible to get a cab? I'd like to get back to my hotel without delay.'

'Of course.' She breathed a sigh of relief as he made no attempt to continue the discussion. 'My own car is not in the city just now, an inconvenience for which I offer my regrets. If you care to take shelter here, in this doorway, I'll get a taxi.'

Gina nodded, too full of unidentified feelings to trust herself to speak. Was she the only person in the world who felt that love was too precious a commodity to cheapen by offering it as a stake in a game where the prize was emotional titillation? For a few brief moments she'd actually managed to persuade herself that there was some kind of special rapport between herself and the man who had kissed her in the semi-darkness with such tender passion. More fool she!

Shivering, she brushed a few drops of rain from her face, glad when Rune returned in a few minutes in the promised taxi. Neither spoke on the journey, but, after wishing her a formal '*Godnat*' on the threshold of the hotel, he added casually, 'I'll pick you up here at nine tomorrow morning and we can decide where to continue our search.'

'That won't be necessary. I'm quite capable of searching for Suzie by myself.' It was the decision she'd made on the silent journey back to the hotel, and one she intended to keep.

'Ten, then, if nine's too early,' he said crisply, 'Whatever our feelings towards each other, it's illogical to allow them to interfere with getting our joint problem solved. You'll realise the sense of that after a good night's sleep.'

On the point of reiterating her decision, Gina hesitated. Why not let him think he'd won the argument? 'All right,' she said wearily, smiling inwardly as she saw the gleam of triumph which lightened his eyes. 'But make it ten.'

It was eight the following morning when she awakened, prompted by the rays of the morning sun playing on her eyelids. Stretching luxuriously, she enjoyed the warm comfort of the bed. Her first priority this morning must be to phone Margaret and tell her she was on Suzie's trail.

With a small sigh of exasperation she thrust her feet to the floor. What a pity she had nothing more positive to tell her mother! At least she could take some comfort from the fact that Rune Christensen was also in the hunt. However annoyed he was going to be with her when he discovered she had no intention of spending the day with him, she was certain that if he found Svend before she found Suzie he would notify her accordingly, if only to ensure Suzie's hasty departure to the UK.

Emerging from beneath the spray of the shower, she dried herself briskly before dressing with impatient fingers. It was a day for jeans and a T-shirt, she decided after a quick look at the sky—a mottled jigsaw of blue and white.

The dining-room was crowded as she made her way to the open buffet table. A babble of voices, predominantly American and German, provided a background hum, while a great number of tables, she observed with some surprise, were occupied by a contingent of Japanese businessmen wearing identical lapel-badges and obviously attending some conference.

The breakfast choice was just as Rune had described the previous evening, she discovered, running jaundiced eyes over the available spread before deciding to settle for orange juice, yoghurt and black coffee. Damn! Why couldn't she put the image of that wretched man out of her mind? Finding space at a recently vacated table, she sat down, staring moodily at her juice. It wasn't as if she was attracted to him as an individual. In fact he embodied everything she disliked in a man—arrogance, a physical appearance which turned female heads engendering conceit, authoritarianism and a complete disregard for the feelings of others. On top of all that, he played the trumpet with all the skill of a modern-day Joshua!

In an effort to disguise the smile which rose unbidden to her lips at her own powerful imagery she ducked her head and dealt with the orange juice. If it hadn't been for Lotta's appearance on the scene, who knew how badly the walls of her own citadel might have been rocked by the forceful vibes he'd transmitted?

Pins and needles tingled at her nerve-endings—sweet Georgina Price indeed! Just for a few seconds she'd fallen for the powerful aphrodisiac of music, her senses sharpened by aquavit and the potent charisma of a man who would stop at nothing to achieve his desired ends! Thank heavens she'd escaped his clutches in time. If Lotta hadn't made her entry on cue and Rune had decided to prolong the specious friendship he had conjured up until she had duly appeared on the scene. . . Despite the warmth of the room Gina shivered.

Resolutely she finished the fragrant coffee before phoning Margaret, giving as optimistic a picture of the situation as possible and promising to keep in touch. The clock in the hotel foyer showed the time as nine-fifteen as she pushed through the doors and walked through the patio. With a detailed map of the city in her shoulder-bag, plus a copy of the tourist board's publication, *Copenhagen This Week*, she was as equipped as anyone to seek out the places to which Suzie would be drawn. Of course there was a very large element of luck involved, but unless or until something better came along it was the only option she had.

It was nearly two in the afternoon when, having watched the changing of the Guard at the Amalienborg Palace, admired the copper spire of the old Stock Exchange formed by the twisted tails of four dragons, gazed in appreciation at the magnificent Gefion's Fountain and paid the customary respects to the statue of the Little Mermaid at the entrance to the harbour, she caught a bus back to the canal district.

Nyhavn, full of character and teeming with life, was just the sort of place that Suzie would love: two rows of picturesque houses flanking either side of a canal which was lined with old fishing boats, their tall masts and graceful rigging moving lazily as the light wind ruffled the water. Behind the beautifully restored façades of the buildings with their smart paint and gabled roofs there was evidence of a rich and varied culture, Gina observed, walking down the crowded cobbled pathway where restaurants and cafés spilled out towards the water's edge. The presence of tattoo shops, 'topless' discothèques which offered dancing and music almost twenty-four hours a day were a reminder that Copenhagen was an active and important port, yet the overall effect was charming and romantic as flowers spilled out of window-boxes and the cafés and restaurants vied with each other to attract custom by the quality of their food and their individual décor.

Walking slowly, she allowed her eyes to roam over the seated lunchers, hoping to catch sight of Suzie's dark curls, but although once or twice her heart leapt to her mouth in anticipation of discovery she was finally forced to admit defeat. Finding an empty space at one of the cafés, she ordered coffee and a *smørrebrød*—a large buttered open sandwich—covered on this occasion with her choice of salmon, smoked eel and shrimp and garnished with a variety of delicious accessories.

By the time she'd finished there was still no sign of Suzie among the strolling couples enjoying the sunshine. So, paying her bill, she decided to make for Gammel Strand and on impulse joined one of the canal tours.

After so much walking, a great deal of it on cobblestones, her feet could do with a rest! Sitting back on her seat, she relaxed as the engine started and the long, low open canal boat passed under the first of the very low bridges which spanned the narrow waterways, and tuned in her ear to the English commentary being given by the boat's guide, mentally turning off when it was followed in French and German to engage in a desultory conversation with a fellow countryman who had chanced to take the place beside her, a pleasant young man attending his first seminar in Denmark.

Well, at least one good thing would come out of this trip, she decided philosophically—she would know a great deal more about Denmark's capital city by the time she returned to England.

It was nearly six-thirty by the time she arrived back at the hotel, having spent more time wandering through Strøget on the way there. It was only as she reached the small turning leading to the patio that she stopped, a momentary apprehension bringing goose-pimples to her skin. Suppose if Rune Christensen was waiting for her? No, that was absurd. Why should he be? Surely he was bright enough to realise that her deliberate snub meant that she didn't want to see him again? Nevertheless it was with a great sense of relief that she found the patio deserted save for a handful of hotel guests drinking beer and enjoying the late afternoon sunshine.

The foyer, too, was empty as she walked across it, nodding to the girl behind the reception desk. Pressing the floor button in the small lift, she wondered where to spend the evening. Returning to the jazz clubs was one option, but Rune had already made attempts to cover that by enlisting the aid of several barmen as well as his friends at Ib's Bar. Besides, the last thing she wanted was to come face to face with Rune again, especially if he was in the arms of a reconciled Lotta!

No. There must be other places in the evening where Suzie might be expected to put in an appearance. Once in the comfort of her room she'd look through her guide again for likely possibilities, she decided.

Thrusting the heavy wooden doors of the lift open as they reached her floor, she precipitated herself into the small lobby from which the corridor to her room led, recoiling in dismay as a tall figure unwound itself from one of the two easy chairs beside a small table graced with a vase of fresh flowers.

Wearing an open-necked shirt in a shade of blue which intensified the colour of his eyes and complemented the width of his shoulders and silver-grey trousers that moulded slim hips before encasing long, muscled legs, Rune Christensen looked like some godly visitor from Asgard—and one bent on vengeance.

CHAPTER SIX

'WHAT are you doing here?' Her body stiff with defiance, Gina confronted Rune, observing the hard muscle twitching spasmodically in the hollow beneath one cheekbone, and his eyes cold and dangerous beneath heavy lids.

'Waiting for you—what else?'

'Since ten o'clock?' She made no attempt to disguise the sarcasm that gave an added cadence to her voice.

'So you did remember our date—you just chose to ignore it?'

She lifted her shoulders in a dismissive shrug, wishing heartily that someone else would make an appearance to lower the tension in the air. But the lift remained silent, the long, winding corridor empty.

'I changed my mind. I preferred to look for Suzie by myself.'

'Did you find her?' His question had the cutting edge of a razor.

'No,' she admitted, refusing to lower her eyes beneath his supercilious gaze. 'How about you? Did you find Svend?'

'Not yet.' His mouth twisted, a flash of antagonism in the depth of his eyes as they dwelt on her challenging face. 'But, believe me, I intend to. The sooner I get him out of the hands of that teenage vixen, the happier I shall be!'

'Suzie isn't——'

'Your sister is a major obstacle in Svend's career,' Rune interrupted her heated retort bluntly, 'and the

71

sooner he's persuaded to abandon her, the better for all of us!'

'At least I can agree with that last sentiment! If it hadn't been for your shiftless nephew, Suzie would be back in England by now, my mother wouldn't be having sleepless nights and I could be in London doing the job for which I'm paid!'

'Ah, yes. Writing pretty words in an attempt to persuade a gullible public to spend their money.' His half-smile taunted her. 'At least you have the consolation of knowing your profession isn't one of life or death for the people you have left in the lurch in your noble search to rescue your innocent sister from her Viking abductor.'

'Not all of us have a vocation to be nurses or doctors.' Gina's eyes sparkled with barely suppressed animosity at his blatant derision. 'In case it's escaped your notice, we all live in a consumer society. We need a healthy economy based on trade in order to finance the service industries, and advertising and promotion are part of the cycle.' She lifted her dark head higher in an unconscious gesture of pride. 'I'm not ashamed of what I do. My job is both creative and informative. I aim to tell the truth, present a product fairly, and please both the advertiser and the prospective purchaser. I feel I have a flair for what I do and I enjoy it!' And if the recession continued much longer she might return to London to find herself looking for some other occupation to keep the roof over her head—but that was her secret.

Allowing some of the built-up tension inside her to dissipate, she forced a mocking smile to her dry lips. 'As a manufacturer yourself you would be more percipient about the role of advertising in selling your product, I would have thought.'

'Perhaps I prefer cold air to hot air,' he suggested

urbanely, his eyes darkening with what could have been amusement at her spirited defence of her career. 'Tell me, how long have you worked for this advertising agency which plays such an important part in the British economy?'

'Long enough to know my own worth,' Gina retorted, irritated by the sardonic gleam in his eyes. 'And I don't see what that has to do with the problem in hand.'

'Perhaps not,' he agreed smoothly. 'But if we're going to spend the evening together I thought it would help if we knew more about each other's backgrounds.'

'Then, as we're not, you won't expect an answer to your question, will you?' she responded brightly. 'Now, if you'll excuse me, I've had a very tiring day and I want to go back to my room and have a shower.'

'Fine by me.' He moved swiftly, opening the door to the corridor and standing back for her to go through. 'I much prefer to discuss our differences in private. 505 is your room number, isn't it?'

Gina stopped where she was, her fingers clenched in the palms of her hand as she fought to control the surge of irritation which threatened to make her lose her temper completely, while Rune's brilliant gaze held her in thrall, intimate, deliberately self-assured. Presumably he had used his wiles on the pretty blonde receptionist on duty to elicit this information, which would explain why he was here on the fifth-floor landing harassing her.

'Whoever gave you that information is guilty of a clear breach of professional behaviour,' she said when she felt able to control the incipient tremor in her voice. 'And, believe me, I shall make a point of reporting it to the hotel manager without delay.'

'No, you won't.' The correction was gentle, the sharpness of his gaze softened by a shadow of some emotion impossible to designate. 'Because I told her we were lovers and you were expecting me, and you have too much compassion in your make-up to get the girl reprimanded when she believed she was acting in your best interests, *min søde* Gina.'

How was it possible he could know her so well after such a short time? Enough to know that her righteous indignation would fade under the realisation that no malice had been intended and no real harm done. But lovers! How dared he use such effrontery?

'So how long *have* you been waiting?' she enquired, refusing to give him the satisfaction of rising to his bait or confirming his accurate character diagnosis.

A nonchalant shrug of shoulders. 'No more than half an hour. How did you enjoy your trip on the canals?'

Guesswork, second sight, or had he actually seen her? Before she had a chance to enquire or even reply to his question, he was speaking again.

'Look, it's absurd to stand here bandying words. Invite me into your room and we can talk in a civilised manner—through the bathroom door if you insist— while you get ready for tonight's date.'

'How many more times do I have to tell you? I have no intention of going anywhere with you tonight, let alone inviting you into my room!' Anger a tight constriction in her throat, Gina took a step through the open door, her fingers clutching the key to her room. If he forced his way in then she would phone Reception and have him ejected!

Moving with a superb masculine grace which suggested the muscular co-ordination of a regular sportsman, Rune side-stepped her, blocking her way, his hand moving swiftly to fasten on her arm. Through the brushed cotton of her sweater she could feel the pressure of his fingers, his touch scorching her as surely as if it had been on her bare skin.

'Take your hands off me!'

'Why?' He smiled slowly, his eyes travelling over her in a way that sent a tremor through her nervous system. 'Last night you appeared to have no qualms about my doing far more intimate things than merely touching your arm.'

'Because I thought. . .' She stopped abruptly. The reliable rhythm of her pulse seemed to have changed in some odd and basic way. How could she tell this impossible Dane that for some wild, unaccountable moment the previous evening, when his mouth had joined with hers, she'd imagined they shared a mutual attraction so powerful that it had overridden any man-made measurement of time or propriety? Particularly because it was only now, when he was so close to her, that every cell of her body was reacting in some primordial, incomprehensible way to his nearness, to the sheer magnetic pull of his very commanding presence, that she had become aware of the fantasy that had consumed her.

'You thought?' he prompted gently, his fingers moving in a gentle caressing movement on the soft fabric of her sweater. 'What exactly did you think, Gina?' There was a breath of laughter in his voice.

Pulling herself together with an effort, she gave him what she hoped was a cool look.

'I wasn't aware of the fact that I was being used to provoke your "lovely Lotta" in an attempt to further your tempestuous love-life! I suggest you find some other gambit to threaten your queen with tonight.'

'A chess player, too!' To her chagrin he smiled approvingly. 'The more I see of you, the more I'm convinced that we have a great deal more in common than being related to a tiresome adolescent. But don't worry, *min kaere*, we have a table for two only, reserved in one of the finest restaurants in Tivoli with an unequalled view over one of the main paths through the gardens.' He paused before adding gently, 'You have heard of Tivoli, I presume?'

Of course she'd heard of Tivoli! The famous amusement park built in the heart of Copenhagen. No, that was an inadequate description. Even before she'd started her hasty research of the locality she'd known the reputation of Tivoli with its lake and gardens, its fountains and arbours, its hundreds of thousands of flickering lamps at night, its pavilions, theatres, restaurants, bandstands—a haven of pleasure and entertainment in a natural setting of great beauty. On her way to the Rådhuspladsen she'd passed its entrance several times, knowing that it must have a high priority in her search for Suzie.

Tonight would be perfect. If the weather pattern was as uncertain as it was in her own country, she should take the opportunity of going there while the sky remained unclouded and the clear air of the city simmered with a body-relaxing warmth. Given the few moments of contemplation she'd wanted, it would probably have been her own choice for the evening. But not in the company of Rune the remorseless!

He was regarding her patiently, not prompting a reply, but still standing close enough to abort any sudden move on her part to escape.

'They have T-shirts in the tourist shops,' she said at last, determined not to show any sign of the enthusiasm bubbling up inside her. 'With a clever little reversal of the name for English tourists—"Tivoli—I lov it!".'

'As most people do—Copenhageners as much as visitors,' Rune agreed calmly. 'So why not join me there tonight in the enchanted garden and form your own opinion?'

Enchanted garden. Gina shivered. Already she was under some malign spell that seemed woven to keep her close to Rune Christensen. Too close. Enchanted gardens she could do without. On the other hand, it was such a likely place for her romantic-minded young sister to frequent, and the sooner she found Suzie, the sooner she could put a stretch of the North Sea between herself and the clear-eyed Scandinavian whose presence she found so unnerving.

'Did it occur to you that I might have made other arrangements?' she said eventually. Having decided to surrender to his plans for the evening—lunch had been a light one and already the pangs of hunger were making themselves felt—she wouldn't do it without a token show of resistance.

'With the young man who had his arm round you in the boat?' She felt his fingers tighten spasmodically on her arm as her mouth opened in utter surprise at his unexpected retort. 'So break them. There's no need for you to pick up strangers to escort you when, as you know, I'm more than willing to do so.'

'For your own purposes!' she flared. Damn him if she would explain that the young man to whom he'd referred had merely been a fellow Briton attending a conference on international computing, that they'd exchanged nothing more than a few polite comments natural to fellow compatriates abroad, and that his arm had been lying across the back of the bench seats and not round her shoulders.

'Of course.' His eyebrows rose in mock surprise that she should question his motives. 'Surely you're old enough to realise that all men have some ulterior motive when they invite a woman out? In this case, the sooner I remove young Svend from Suzie the siren, and make him aware of his responsibilities towards his parents and his own future, the sooner I can resume a normal life! So you have a choice. Either I accompany you to your room and wait while you have your shower and do whatever else you feel necessary before we leave, or I wait here, in the lobby, and you give me your word that you will join me within the hour.'

Some choice! And he'd deliberately misinterpreted her meaning about his own purposes. He must have known she was referring to the game he was playing with Lotta! She met his eyes without flinching, a mutinous sparkle enlivening the depths of her own grey gaze. There was a third alternative. She could choose to go to her room alone, then break her word. Oaths made under threat weren't morally enforceable, were they? On the other hand that would mean she would have to spend the rest of the night in her room with the door locked while he mounted guard outside, forgoing both the pleasure of quelling her hunger pangs and, much more important, a very real opportunity of fulfilling her original quest.

'One hour, then,' she said coldly, glancing down at her watch to check the time.

'I have your word?' He was taking no chances as his clear gaze dared her to lie.

She sighed, defeated and resigned. 'You have my word.'

An hour later she was keeping it, sharing the small lift with him, keeping her face averted from the complacent look that painted his prepossessing face with an irritating blandness. Her first surprise on reaching the street was to discover that Rune had a sleek dark blue Mercedes parked outside.

'I collected it from my house this afternoon,' he explained laconically.

'House?' She betrayed her curiosity before she had time to think better about appearing interested in his personal life.

'Mmm.' He didn't seem in the least affected by her inquisitiveness. 'The Copenhagen apartment is a recent acquisition. I've owned a house on the coast for a year or so, and decided to leave the car in the garage there when I went to the Middle East.' He waited while she dealt competently with the seatbelt. 'As a matter of fact it was while I was crossing one of the canals on my way back here that I happened to catch sight of you and your friend. That's when I decided to gamble on the chance that you'd soon be returning to the hotel to freshen up before the start of the evening. Fortunately my instinct proved correct.'

It was still daylight as Rune, having parked the car and guided her across the road, stood back to let her precede him through the Tivoli turnstiles. Immediately she was conscious of something different in the atmosphere, a feeling of expectation linked to a pervading harmony. There were many other people around from every age-group, yet the overall impression she received was one of unhurried leisure.

Shafts of sunlight gleamed through the avenue of trees, warming the air so that she felt no need to wear the jacket she had brought with her as a precaution against the temperamental nature of Danish weather, holding it casually instead over one arm, perfectly comfortable in the same linen dress she had worn the previous evening. Only tonight she'd left her hair loose, brushing it straight back from her forehead and letting it fall in its natural soft waves to her shoulders. Every so often the light wind teased it away from her ears, revealing her favourite earrings as they swung against its soft darkness.

Beside her Rune looked what he was, she thought—purposeful and determined, master of his own destiny, the skin of his golden jaw so smooth that he must have shaved again before coming to pick her up, his hair gleaming in molten strands as the sunlight played on it.

When he reached for her free hand, clasping it in his

own, it was as if she'd touched a metal surface after walking on a nylon carpet—the shock of contact almost painful in its suddenness.

'If you're going to enjoy Tivoli as it deserves to be enjoyed, I think for tonight at least we should call a truce,' he suggested, apparently unaware of her intense reaction to his touch, as they walked past the Pantominteatret, where a performance of the traditional Italian pantomime was taking place on the open-air stage.

Conscious of his questioning gaze resting on her profile, Gina offered him a tentative smile. 'Why not?' she replied, and was rewarded by the slight extra pressure he applied to her hand.

Why not, indeed? Perhaps a little fantasy was just what she needed, she decided, mentally preparing to suspend disbelief and abandon herself to whatever awaited her. Marcus had said she was too introverted and frigid to have the vaguest idea how to find, let alone enjoy, the pleasures of life. If she was to indulge in escapism, surely here would be as good a place as any?

Only a few metres through its portals and already the spell was reaching her, soothing her jagged nerves. A few more metres and she was faced with a panorama of colourful flower-beds surrounding a small lake where, as a centre-piece, air bubbled through a series of glass tubes of varying diameter and height to make an eye-catching display.

As they strolled deeper into the gardens she became aware that the Pantominteatret was by no means the only form of free entertainment, as their progress led them from one area of performance to another. On one concert bandstand a quintet played classical music, on another a small jazz band enlivened the air, to the delight of the small groups of people who stood listening. Facing a large lawn was yet another open-air theatre where acrobats performed. Exotic edifices enhanced the impression of an *Arabian Nights* baroque extravaganza captured and reborn in a setting of Nature at its most verdant. A truly fairy-tale mirage that tugged at the heartstrings.

They'd been strolling through the individual gardens within the whole for more than two hours, while Rune told her about the traditions of the gardens and how, despite attempts at imitation, they remained unique in Europe—if not the world—before they reached the area set aside for the funfair and he suggested she might like a ride on some of the attractions.

'No, thank you. I'm too old and too big for the things I like, and the others terrify me!'

She shuddered as the switchback roared overhead, but stood watching as a small train meandered through a series of paths, and laughed at the joyful screams of the children on the dodgems. When Rune successfully tried his luck at a shooting gallery and invited her to choose which prize she wanted, she selected a paperweight in the form of the Little Mermaid sitting on her rock. Back in London on her desk, it would be an everlasting reminder of this evening. Whether she would live to regret her choice, only time would tell.

For the moment her critical faculties seemed to have deserted her. Even the tall Dane beside her no longer aroused her guarded antipathy, she realised with something like shock. A warning pulse quickened within her body, but there was also a kind of excitement, a high tension which disrupted her normal caution.

They'd just walked full circle past the famous Tivoli lake with the much photographed and traditionally Danish Old Ferry Inn jutting out into its depths, and through the sunken garden, back to the bubble fountain, when the lights were switched on.

The time had passed so quickly that she hadn't

realised how late it was, or that the daylight had faded to dusk. A gasp of delight escaped her lips as instantly the gardens assumed a new and spellbinding dimension: thousands of light bulbs springing to life, outlining domes and minarets, and other graceful exotic images of the architects' imagination.

'Well—what do you think? Are you glad you came?' Rune's soft question pierced her enchantment.

'How could I be otherwise?' she responded obliquely. Of course she was glad she'd had the opportunity to savour this experience, but it was also curiously frightening, because it was stirring something deep inside her that she hadn't realised existed. It was like a dream, too good to be true and never likely to be recaptured.

'Let's eat, then.' Rune had given her a sharp glance as she replied, but then appeared to accept her question as an affirmative, as he took her firmly by the arm to lead her into his chosen restaurant.

Their table was in an area resembling a glass veranda, every other one of the large plate-glass windows slid back so that the mild night air, scented with flowers, wafted over them. Subtle lamps gleamed on pink-clothed tables, each with its own vase of flowers. The menu was extensive, the service unobtrusive and efficient.

'I'm afraid I can't suggest a Danish wine, since our climate doesn't favour the cultivation of the grape, but we import some of the best of our neighbours' efforts. Do you have a preference?' Rune handed her the wine list.

'That's something our two countries have in common,' she commented, casting an eye over what was available. 'An uncertain climate—but we do have some promising vineyards in the south, and British wine is already being marketed in small quantities at home. If our climate continues to be as mild as it has been for the last couple of winters we may yet challenge our French and German competitors!' She handed the list back to him. 'Something white and dry, preferably, but I'll leave the choice to you.'

'Right.' He indicated a bin number to the attendant waiter before turning his attention back to her.

'Shall we drink to the success of our joint project?' He waited until the waiter had filled their glasses before suggesting the toast.

Chablis, pale as a northern sunrise, clear as Danish crystal. Gina nodded, lifting her glass to her lips.

'Skål!' Rune's voice, low and demanding, stilled her hand as he held his own glass towards her.

'Skål.' Obediently she returned the gesture, meeting his mesmeric gaze, feeling the power of his appraisal bathe her in a tingling aura before taking a deep, refreshing swallow. Remembering what he had taught her, she commanded her eyes to meet his yet again before replacing her glass on the table.

She was trembling, perhaps because she'd suddenly remembered that the origin of the toast she had just drunk lay in the Viking custom of saluting each other by drinking from the skulls of their enemies.

She only knew that from the moment she had stepped on to Danish soil she'd been caught up in circumstances over which she had no control, but which appeared moment by moment to be leading her further from her original purpose.

Suzie! With a start of shame she realised that she'd scarcely paid her sister a moment's thought since entering the gardens. She could have walked past her a dozen times and never even noticed her, so intent had she been in enjoying her own experience, so wrapped up in the ambience that Rune had encouraged with his own participation of the pleasures around them.

In penance she turned her head towards the open window, searching the small groups of people who ambled along the path for a familiar face. She didn't deserve such miracles, and neither, did it seem, would she be granted one.

CHAPTER SEVEN

'TELL me more about Suzie.' Rune must have read her guilt and disappointment as she turned her head away from him. 'This friction between her and your mother—was it really important or just a manifestation of teenage rebellion?'

'I think it was just a build-up of ongoing tension between them,' Gina admitted unhappily. 'I doubt if Suzie's any worse than the average teenager. She's tender-hearted, generous, vivacious but at the same time she likes to have her own way. As for Margaret— well——' She paused, not wanting to be disloyal, then continued as Rune gave her a quick nod of encouragement. 'She's very possessive, and I'm afraid Suzie's not mature enough to be able to understand or cope with the situation.'

'Whereas you are?' A cynical sparkle lit his eyes for a moment.

Gina shrugged. 'I don't have to be. Margaret and I aren't close. In fact we rarely see each other.'

'Only when she needs something from you, perhaps?' Rune smiled without mirth, his eyes coolly calculating on her pale face. 'Why? I wonder. Or could it be that you were the first rebel in the household and that Suzie's only following your example?'

If Rune had set out deliberately to enrage her he couldn't have chosen a better way. How dared he surmise her behaviour when he hadn't the faintest idea of what her childhood had been like?

'Bad guess!' Dark and stormy, her eyes flashed a lightning spear of rebuke at his bland face. 'You have to be a member of a household before you can rebel against it, and that's something I never was! From the moment I was born I was a nuisance. The only reason Margaret went through with the pregnancy was because my father hoped I'd be a boy. When I wasn't he lost all interest in me. As for Margaret—well, she'd always fancied herself accompanying my father round the world on his tours. Oh, he didn't earn that much playing golf, but he was lucky enough to have a substantial private income to indulge his sport. My arrival put paid to her travels—at least for the first couple of years.'

Horrified at her loss of composure, she tried to regain it. It wasn't as if she even liked this man enough to care a damn for his opinion of her! Giving a hard laugh, she held out her empty glass towards Rune. 'May I?'

'Of course.' Rune filled her glass, watching her as she half emptied it in one long swallow, waiting until she replaced it on the table before enquiring mildly, 'Then what happened?'

'Baby-sitters, temporary care by distant relatives and friends who wanted to earn pin-money. Later on— boarding schools. . .'

She halted as Rune's hand sought hers across the table, covering it with overt compassion.

'Oh, there's no need to feel sorry for me!' Quickly she rejected his overture of comfort. She'd never asked for nor expected pity. 'I wasn't neglected in any way. In fact I had an education many a girl would envy—all the extras, you know.' From somewhere she dredged up a brilliant smile, still angry she had allowed this aggravating man to get beneath her defences. 'Not many girls leave school not only with good exam passes but also with competence certificates in horse-riding, swimming and lace-making!'

'Lace-making! Now that does impress me!' He was laughing at her, but not unkindly. 'And where does Suzie fit into this idyllic picture?'

'I was eight when she was born. Of course I didn't know it at the time, but by then my mother and father's marriage was showing cracks. Margaret hadn't found the glamour she'd sought and Campion, my father, was bored by her following him around. I think he saw her role as staying at home, keeping a base in England for him when he decided to retire. Suzie was the result of one last effort on my mother's behalf to produce the son that Campion wanted. When it failed she virtually gave up, and accepted the facts for what they were.'

She paused to take another sip of wine, conscious of Rune's unremitting interest in her recital. Why was she unburdening her heart to him? It was the first time she'd ever spoken about her early life to anyone. The irony was that those who had observed it had considered her spoiled and stuck-up. On the few occasions she'd spent holidays at home she'd been a social outcast among her contemporaries. None had guessed the desolation she'd experienced or how she'd built a protective screen around her emotions, determined that neither tears nor anger would betray her inner pain.

'And how did that decision affect you?'

Glancing up, startled, she met Rune's clear eyes narrowed in speculation, wondering just how much he was able to discern beneath the camouflage she'd thought she'd assumed.

'Not at all really.' Deliberately she kept her tone light. 'The last thing my mother wanted was a child underfoot while she was dealing with a baby. I was eight when I went to proper boarding school for the first time. And, although I did go home for a few holidays, most I seem to remember were spent elsewhere with friends or at special holiday camps that some of the other boarders went to.'

'But not Suzie,' Rune said drily.

'No, not Suzie,' she agreed with a small humourless smile. 'Once Margaret had decided not to follow my father around she devoted all her energies to Suzie. Oh, I don't think it was because she particularly disliked me or anything like that. . .' Despite the effort she had made, she found it difficult to swallow the lump which rose in her throat. 'It was just that we were strangers and awkward with each other, whereas Suzie was malleable. At least——' she gave a rueful laugh '——she was for the first twelve years of her life. After that things changed!'

'And after you left school?' Rune seemed singularly uninterested in her sister's career.

'University, a communications and media course and a lucky break with a first-rate London advertising agency. For the first couple of years I shared a flat with a friend, then my paternal grandmother died and unexpectedly left me a small legacy. With the help of that and an increasing salary I was able to get a mortgage on my own small flat just outside London.' She cast away the unwelcome thought that if she was made redundant she would have to find new work immediately or forfeit that small oasis of security she'd won for herself.

'You live there alone?' Rune's tone was casual, but there was nothing lazy about the way he leaned across the table towards her.

Startled by his temerity, her dark eyebrows lifted in assumed mockery. 'What would you expect?' No way was she going to admit her emotional isolation to this self-possessed Nordic tormentor. If she couldn't fool him, then she would lie.

'At first glance?' A cynical sparkle for a moment lit

up his eyes. 'That you shared your life with at least one ardent and devoted partner. . .' His gaze pinned her, intimate, all-knowing. 'But after knowing you for as long as I have——'

'Two days!' she interposed, trying to lace her voice with sarcasm, furious when she heard her protest come out breathy and shaken.

'Long enough to form an educated opinion, *min skat*——'

'Must you call me that ridiculous name?' Anything to divert his attention, to prevent him from labelling her with the cruel names she'd last heard on Marcus's tongue.

'You prefer the English translation?' He laughed, his teeth glinting white, 'Very well, *my treasure*, but the answer's still the same. I think you are totally untouched by the hand of love. Bruised a little by poor imitations maybe. Like the Sleeping Beauty, you are still waiting for your prince to come and awaken you.'

'You couldn't be more wrong!' She rose to her feet, pushing her chair back determinedly. 'As a matter of fact I've been living for the past two years with a wonderful man. His name is Marcus. . .' Now she'd spoken his name she was committed, intent on preserving her dignity: making the point to her attractive companion that, whatever he might be thinking, she wasn't in the market for love—or the poor reproduction of that emotion that a lot of men produced in the pursuit of sexual thrills. Neither was she available to be cast as the 'other woman' to further his own tumultuous affair with Lotta! 'We plan on getting married in the near future!' she lied flagrantly.

'My congratulations.' Rune's tone was bland, his expression suggesting that if it hadn't been impolite he would have challenged her rash assertion.

Thankfully the arrival of the waiter with their main

course gave her time to treat his unwarranted reaction with the disdain it deserved. The menu was extensive, and since her taste was catholic she had had no hesitation in asking Rune for his recommendation. Now, as the waiter served them both with salmon poached in white wine, dressed with a spicy sauce and served with salad and new potatoes, she felt her mouth watering in anticipation of the meal.

'And you're convinced you will be able to persuade Suzie to go back to England?' It was several minutes into the meal before Rune broke the silence between them.

Gina sighed. It had been the question she had been pondering herself. Although she and Rune had exchanged verbal descriptions of their respective relations the previous evening, words were no substitute for flesh and blood. Svend, she knew, was blond and blue-eyed, but did he have the powerful charisma of his uncle? And, if so, would Suzie be so blinded by it that no appeal to her would prevail?

'The last two years we've grown really close,' she said at last. 'When things got too hot for her at home with Margaret she'd often spend a night at my flat cooling off.' She met Rune's steady gaze with a touch of hauteur. 'She's not the amoral teenage flirt you've labelled her, Rune! Yes, I'm optimistic about making her see that her best interests lie in returning home to finish her exams, but a lot is going to depend on your nephew—how deeply she's involved with him and his attitude towards her.' She paused, before adding accusingly, 'Besides, we have to find them first, and I'm not sure sitting here indulging ourselves is a very effective way of doing that—particularly as my time in Denmark is limited!'

'How limited?' His eyebrows drew together in a frown.

She shrugged. 'I must go back on Sunday at the latest.'

'And tomorrow's Thursday.' His blue gaze flickered over her tense features. 'Marcus keep you on a short leash, does he? Not surprising, if you're in the habit of picking up strange young men on canal boats and letting them cuddle you!'

Dignity decreed that she stay silent in the face of such provocation, but the adrenalin was dancing in her nervous system, demanding action. 'I did not pick up anyone,' she declared vehemently. 'The young man you saw merely exchanged a few words in English with me, and his arm was on the back of the seat—not cuddling me! In any case my personal life has nothing to do with you,' she retorted, stung by his overriding air of masculine superiority.

'Wrong, *min kaere* Gina! I can assure you that my concern for Svend is as great as yours for Suzie, and I'm not going to allow you to wriggle out of your commitments because, rightly or wrongly, your lover doesn't trust you out of his sight.'

'You have a way of stopping me?' she asked with cool cynicism, fighting down a wild desire to laugh hysterically. If only Rune knew the truth about herself and Marcus! 'I'd be interested to know how.'

'Try to leave before I'm ready to let you go and you'll find out!' His head went back and he laughed at her mutinous expression, the glint in his eyes deepening, before leaning forward again and addressing her with quiet insistence. 'Listen to me, Gina. Hanne and Jens always hoped that Svend would join them on their farm, but when it became clear that his interests lay in constructional engineering they gladly supported him, despite their disappointment and the sacrifices they had to make.' He gave a short, harsh laugh. 'After all, it was only history repeating itself.'

'Meaning?' Sensing she was about to be taken further into Rune's confidence, Gina encouraged him gently, forgetting her previous animosity at his high-handedness.

A rueful smile twisted his mouth. 'The farm originally belonged to our parents; like Hanne and Jens, they hoped their only son would take over from them, and, like Svend, I too decided that my career lay elsewhere.'

'And they supported you in the same way?' she asked gently.

'Yes.' His face grew still as a shadow of pain darkened his eyes. 'Unfortunately, they were both drowned in a ferry disaster in the Greek islands while I was still at university. The first holiday abroad they'd ever had.' His mouth twisted bitterly. 'So they never lived long enough to know I had justified their faith in me.'

Unable to find the right words, Gina moved her hand impulsively across the table and touched his fingers with her own, unconsciously reciprocating the gesture he had made to her earlier. The difference was that he accepted her attempt at consolation, taking her palm between both of his own hands, holding it gently and meeting her compassionate gaze with the glimmer of a smile.

'The farm had been left to Hanne. She was ten years older than me and already married to Jens, himself the youngest son of a neighbouring farmer, without property of his own. They both swore it would always remain my home while I wanted it, and so it did. I owe them more than money can pay, Gina, and finding Svend and trying to talk some sense into him is just one small thing I can do. Fortunately, my deadline is a little longer than yours. I have another seven days before Jens's cousin arrives from the States and finds his would-be protégé has been seduced into giving him the cold shoulder.'

Sadly Gina shook her head. 'I'm sure if Suzie realised the seriousness of it. . .' She paused, biting her lip. Perhaps neither knew of the other's commitments. Angrily she tore her hand away from Rune's clasp and slammed it palm-down on the table. 'Oh, this is an impossible situation!'

'Not necessarily.' His cool, level gaze was disturbing. 'While you were following your own pursuits this morning, I set a few more wheels in motion. I doubt either can afford to stay at a hotel and I know for a fact that they're not at any of the local hostels; neither, I have been reliably informed, have they put in an appearance at the local "hippie" compound. That suggests they are staying with friends or acquaintances Svend has in the city, and that is the premise I'm having investigated at the moment.'

'You've hired an enquiry agent?' Gina's voice rose in amazement as, uncertain whether to be horrified or impressed, she met his smug expression.

'Let's just say I've got the matter in hand, hmm?' He beckoned the waiter and received a menu. 'Now, what would you like for dessert?'

'Just coffee will be fine,' she said weakly. 'Black, please.' Hastily she searched for her purse in her bag, recalling part of their earlier conversation when he had been escorting her around the park. 'Didn't you say the fireworks begin at a quarter to midnight? It's already twenty to.' She was speaking too quickly, her heart hammering in response to the lies she had told, all her defences raised against a potential enemy. 'Oh, and by the way, this meal is on me.' She'd found her wallet of credit cards and flourished it under his nose, every fibre of her being poised to defy him if he tried to deny her the right to pay.

For a moment she thought she was going to have a battle on her hands, then he relaxed, holding up his palms in a gesture of peace.

'If that's what you want, *min skat*. But be assured, I had no intention of trying to buy your favours with the price of a meal.'

'Just my co-operation in furthering your intrigue with Lotta, no doubt?' she suggested wearily. 'Look, Rune, you footed the bill for yesterday's entertainment. Today it's my turn. I prefer not to be under any obligation to you.'

His light eyes mirrored anger in the hard framework of his face. 'You insult my hospitality and your own worth if you really suppose moral blackmail was my aim. The salmon was delicious, I agree, but hardly sufficient incentive to encourage you to act against your will, I would have thought?'

Gina met his glowering appraisal unrepentantly. 'I just wanted to make my position clear to avoid misunderstandings.'

'Of which it appears you are more guilty than I, *min skat*.' He was controlling his voice to an even conversational tone, using the endearment sarcastically, as if he found it difficult to disguise the build-up of tension which tightened his jaw. 'Whatever intrigue there was between Lotta Petterson and myself died slowly and painfully and has been extinct for much longer than the six months we have gone our separate ways.'

'That's not how she sees it!' She could have bitten her tongue the moment the words left her mouth. His sordid affairs were none of her concern provided she wasn't being asked to play the part of catalyst.

'And you prefer her version to mine?' He smiled slowly, his eyes dwelling on her in a way which sent the warm blood pouring into her face.

'I don't have your version,' Gina justified herself hotly. 'Neither am I interested in it.'

'You prefer to make an uninformed judgement?'

'Lotta did inform me,' she returned, her cool voice in direct contrast to her flushed complexion. 'I'm fully conversant with "love-games". If that's what turns you on that's fine by me, but please leave me out of them. If you want to inflame Lotta's jealousy I'm sure you know a lot of other women who would be only too willing to oblige you.'

'Precisely.' There was a deeper timbre to his voice, but his shrug was light, his shoulders moving almost imperceptibly beneath the stretch of pale blue cotton which emphasised their broadness. 'So why would I choose you? Why would I pretend to involve myself romantically with a woman whose sister has already wreaked such havoc in my family, hmm?'

He rose to his feet, making it clear the question was rhetorical, as Gina, feeling as humiliated as if he had actually slapped her face, tried to hide her chagrin by swallowing the remains of her coffee.

'*Kom*!' He moved behind her chair easing it out as she stood up. 'Or we shall miss the beginning of the display.'

Fifteen minutes to midnight and the night sky formed a black velvet background to a celebration of sound and colour. With no pause between the fountains of rainbow brilliance illuminating the darkness, Gina found herself holding her breath as the spectacle exploded far above her head. She was no ingénue, to gape like a child at its first Guy Fawkes night, but the sheer volume of erupting sound and colour held her in its thrall, her face as rapt as those of the silent crowds around her.

It was only when the colours gave way to plain gold before subsiding into diminishing fountains of silver that she realised she had moved closer to Rune, seeking instinctive protection against the sharp noise of the exploding rockets and that he had gathered her to his strong male body, pinning her to his side by the power of his arm, his hand firmly pressed against her waist.

Fifteen minutes and it was all over, leaving her hungry for more.

'Time to go.' Rune's mouth brushed against her ear, whispering the words.

Embarrassed by his closeness, which admittedly she had encouraged, she pulled herself away. 'So soon?' Disappointment was a hard knot in her chest. 'Is that all?'

'Until the day after tomorrow as far as the fireworks are concerned. We can always come back again then.'

'No, that won't be possible. . .' Still smarting from his snub and his scathing reference to Suzie, she found her mind was made up.

'Why?'

The air between them suddenly seemed static, as she fought for the words to justify her decision. From that very first meeting Rune had projected his own image of her over the reality. He'd pictured her as a woman willing to trade physical favours in exchange for her goals. Even when she'd explained who she was, his opinion hadn't changed. As far as he was concerned, both she and her sister were two of a kind—cheap and unprincipled, living for the moment, regardless of who got hurt in the process. Why else would he read so much into her innocent conversation with a stranger, or casually lie about their being lovers to the hotel receptionist?

Some of the blame was undoubtedly her own because of her mindless response to his kiss at Ib's Club. But he should have realised she'd been carried away by the atmosphere, and the unexpected potency of the aquavit.

Now it was clear he had no real need of her assistance despite his claim to the opposite. The investigation he'd instigated would, by its nature and scope, prove far more efficient than anything either of them could do alone or in tandem. So why was he insisting she continue to go around with him? Only one answer still made sense. Lotta. Despite his assertion to the contrary. There'd been a fault in her original logic which he'd seized upon, but she was already beginning to see the fallacy. Why hurt another girl by pretending an interest he didn't feel when she, Gina, was already on the scene—a woman for whose family he only felt contempt and whose imminent departure was already planned?

'Why, Gina?' he prompted again softly as she tried to arrange her jumbled thoughts to give a reason without betraying how deeply hurt she felt.

She managed a careless movement of her shoulders. 'I would have thought it was obvious. Since you now have the matter under such efficient control, there's no point in our wasting any more time together. I'm sure your company is suffering from your absence, and I'm quite capable of sightseeing on my own.' The way he was regarding her was hardly encouraging, but she persevered, trying to bring an air of insouciance to her voice. 'Hopefully your bloodhounds will be able to run the truants down before Sunday, in which case I'd appreciate your contacting me at the hotel.'

'And if they don't?'

'As I said—I have a job in London to do. Since you're so well organised I'm happy to leave the matter in your hands. I'll give you my home telephone number, and if you don't find them until after I've returned, and you're not successful in persuading Suzie to go back to England, all I ask is that you let me know where I can contact her. If talking to her on the phone doesn't work then I'll have to reconsider my position.'

For a few moments Rune regarded her in silence, a slight smile playing round his strong mouth, then he asked softly, 'What happened to our truce?'

'It ended when the clock struck twelve.'

Around them the crowds were thinning. If only she could turn her back on the golden Dane whose gaze still ensnared her, lose herself in the masses and find her own way back to the hotel, but she was held where she stood by invisible chains.

'Wrong fairy-tale, sweetheart,' he chided gently. 'And I've no intention of allowing you to give me the slip tonight. Quite apart from anything else, I have a business proposition to put to you. An opportunity I believe an ambitious person like yourself will find too good to resist.'

CHAPTER EIGHT

'EXACTLY what is this business proposition?'

Gina had remained silent after Rune's surprise announcement, allowing him to conduct her through the gates and across the road to the Mercedes. Now, as the large car purred into movement, she sent him a tentative look. She'd made one bad mistake in her life, and she wasn't about to make another! On the other hand, if he really had anything constructive to say to her she couldn't allow phantom fears to deny her the opportunity of listening to him. Besides, her curiosity was well and truly awakened.

'It's quite simple, really.' He slanted her a quick look. 'As you know, my company manufactures heating and ventilating equipment. The greater part of our business is commercial, of course, but recently we've branched out into the domestic market with an air-conditioning unit which is comparatively easy to install and cheap to operate. Our main European markets would appear to be around the Mediterranean, but with statistics showing that northern European summers are apparently becoming warmer I've decided to launch our system in the United Kingdom as well.'

'I see.' Intrigued despite herself, Gina half turned in her seat to regard his classic profile. 'But what has this to do with me?'

'Isn't it obvious? I shall need a first-class advertising agency which can identify the main market and come up with a good campaign to target it, woo it with words and obtain a high conversion rate of sales.'

Excitement flickered inside her like a random spark

99

that found itself landing in a pile of dry autumn leaves as she hardly dared consider the possibilities and what they might mean for her.

'You mean you would want a British agency?'

'We might all be one big European family,' he returned drily. 'But that doesn't mean we don't still retain our national idiosyncrasies. Time is at a premium because I want a full launch in time for next spring, and I prefer to use an agency which knows its market intimately.'

'You mean Grantham and Marsh?' It was too good to be true. Despite a reputation for excellent work on the relatively small number of accounts they handled, they had no international reputation and certainly wouldn't be quoted among the top twenty of British advertising agencies as far as billings were concerned. 'But you don't know anything about them!'

'On the contrary,' Rune corrected smoothly. 'I know a great deal about them. I'm aware of the accounts they've handled successfully and also the fact that, owing to the recent recession and not to any fault of their own, they've been seriously affected by the cutback in promotion budgets of several of their larger clients.'

'You mean you've been investigating them?' Gina's brow creased in a frown. Coincidences did happen, but not of this magnitude! A nasty suspicion presented itself to her as Rune drove into the courtyard outside his flat, parking the car neatly. 'You checked up on me!' Her voice rose angrily. 'You actually rang my employers and ask questions about me! How dare you?'

'Daring had very little to do with it. It was hardly a hazardous undertaking. In fact it was very enlightening. I spoke to a charming fellow, name of Sebastian Grantham. . .'

Oh, dear God, the chairman himself!

'He was very complimentary about your work.' Rune unfastened his seatbelt. 'Said you were creative and imaginative, had a distinct flair for words, kept in touch with the common man, were immensely popular with your colleagues and on top of all that delivered your copy promptly.'

'He had no right to discuss me with you!' Her face taut with anger, Gina's fingers trembled uncontrollably as she fumbled with the unfamiliar fastening of the seatbelt.

'Allow me.' Rune brushed her hand and competently released her. 'Since we're obviously about to enter a discussion on ethics, may I suggest it might be more comfortable to do so in my apartment over a cup of coffee and a glass of aquavit?'

'As far as I'm concerned you can keep your coffee and your aquavit.' She was pleased with the way she kept her voice low and controlled. The last thing she wanted was to attract the attention of the neighbours. Almost the last thing, she amended silently. The very last thing she wanted was to go up to Rune's apartment and drink any more of that transmogrifying liquid that already had so much to answer for!

She stumbled out of the car only to find that Rune had been quicker, waiting for her to emerge, offering her his supporting arm as her ankle momentarily twisted on the cobblestones, causing her to utter a sharp cry of distress. Strange, she thought crossly, that the Copenhageners weren't all wearing ankle bandages, but then they'd been born to the decorative but tricky pavements and attuned their footwear accordingly.

'And my advertising campaign?' Rune enquired gently, apparently in no way put out by her castigation. Momentarily bereft of speech as the sharp pain in her

ankle began to subside, Gina could only glare at him.
'Because if that's so it's my duty to tell you that your
Sebastian is going to be very disappointed. He—um—
he appointed you as his special envoy, you see—gave
you *carte blanche* as far as time was concerned; in fact
he insisted that your entire stay here from day one
should be regarded as being on company business.'

'He's not *my* Sebastian,' she protested wildly as her
mind strove to deal with this new complication. 'And I
don't believe a word of this! If it were true he would
have telexed my hotel.'

'I'm sure he has. The message probably arrived a
few minutes after we left. Now are you coming with
me, or not?'

'Will you drive me back to my hotel?' She knew the
answer even before she asked the question, so when
the blond head shook in negation she wasn't surprised.

'Then it seems I have no option,' she told him stiffly.
'Am I to be allowed to phone for a cab from your
apartment?'

He considered her gravely. 'After I've examined
your ankle for damage, put a crêpe bandage round it if
necessary, and discussed my proposed project a little
further, you may certainly phone for a cab if you wish,
although I shall be happy to drive you back myself at
that stage.'

She hesitated for barely a moment before nodding
her head in affirmation. Although she had accused
Rune of lying, some deep intuition told her he had
spoken nothing but the truth. He had certainly
researched Grantham and Marsh and the testimonial
Sebastian had purportedly given her was in line with
the high regard in which she had been told she was
held by the company, although she'd hardly expected
to be given such a glowing recommendation.

Limping slightly, she entered the lift, far more

disturbed by the weight of Rune's arm around her waist than the quickly diminishing pain in her ankle, but unwilling to dispense with the former in case she exacerbated the latter. Heavens! What a memory the man must have. She'd only mentioned the agency's name once the previous evening, but he'd recalled it. Probably making a mental note of it, already determined to check out that she was who she claimed to be, and not Lotta's mischievous accomplice. By evading him earlier that morning she'd played into his hands, at the same time both increasing his suspicions and giving him the best part of the day to allay them. Despite her natural antagonism because he hadn't accepted her word alone, some part of her couldn't help feeling a grudging admiration for his thoroughness.

'Let me see.'

No sooner had she sunk down on one of the chesterfields than he was hunkering down in front of her, lifting her injured foot to rest on his knee, removing the shoe and gently touching the nylon-covered flesh beneath the delicate ankle-bone. 'Is this where it hurts?'

'Originally, but it's improving by the moment, thank you.' She pulled her foot from his knee, too conscious of the firm muscle of his leg beneath the sole and the gentle probing of his long fingers to find the examination anything but acutely embarrassing. 'Probably just a stretched tendon,' she offered matter-of-factly, drawing on a previous experience suffered in her youth as she leant forward, anxious to replace her shoe.

'Probably,' he agreed mildly. 'Here—allow me.' He slid the low-heeled court shoe into place, lifting his hands in simulated amazement. 'Good heavens! It fits! It must be the right fairy-tale after all!'

'Very amusing!' It was hard to suppress an instinctive

smile at his expression, the almost boyish gleam of mischief which sparkled in his eyes, but she managed it.

The smile died from his face, as with a lithe rearrangement of his limbs he twisted around to sit beside her. 'You're angry with me because I checked up on your background?'

She made no answer, letting him read her opinion from the scornful lift of her eyebrows, not trusting herself to speak. Neither would she tell him that half her anger was against herself because of her delayed reaction to his first humiliating kiss which must have hardened his suspicions of her.

'Put yourself in my place, *min søde*,' he exhorted quietly. 'I arrive home after an absence of four weeks to discover that my nephew, my only sister's eldest child, has apparently eloped with some teenage siren, to the distress of his parents and the possible detriment of his career. Naturally I wanted to find out more about her family.'

'I'd already told you all you needed to know!'

'And I needed to confirm it!' His voice had a sharp edge of anger to it. 'Women like you have a way with words that tends to blur the truth. I needed to satisfy myself that Suzie was indeed your sister and that there was no conspiracy between you.'

Gina's eyes widened in disbelief, her worst fears realised. 'You're paranoid!'

'Forget the psychological labels.' He dismissed her accusation with a brief gesture of one hand. 'Let's just say I'm sceptical where the fairer sex are concerned.'

'And that's another thing!' she rounded on him, a flush of temper staining her high cheekbones. 'What exactly do you mean by "women like me"? In your estimation, what kind of woman am I?'

For a few moments she thought he had no intention

of answering her as her whole being quivered with indignation that he should have the nerve to pass judgement on her when not even her closest friends knew her innermost thoughts and longings. Then he gave a soft, deprecatory laugh.

'Beautiful, desirable. . .the kind of woman who only has to walk into a room in order to arouse the predator inside every man there.'

Gina recoiled, her mind spinning as his blue eyes, brilliant and intense beneath brows drawn together in thoughtful consideration, travelled over her astonished face. He was mocking her—he had to be! But even that knowledge didn't prevent a wave of fearful anticipation washing through her body.

'That's nonsense!' She'd meant her tone to be clipped and dismissive, but even to her own ears it sounded slurred and indistinct as she made a mental attempt to regain conscious control over the increased rhythm of her heart. 'You were talking about a business proposition. . .' Desperately she tried to get the conversation back on an impersonal footing.

'Later. There is something more important that concerns me.' The intensity of his gaze mesmerised her. 'Why do you continue to pretend that there is nothing more between us than a common interest in two wayward adolescents?'

'Rune. . .' It was half-protest, half-exhilaration as he obliterated the space between them, taking her in his arms to pull her body hard against his own. 'Please don't start anything.' Weakly she tried to push him away, her face strained in the dim glow from the shaded wall lights, terrified as much by her own emotions as by his very physical presence.

'It's already started,' he murmured, his mouth against her cheek, his hands sliding in gentle caresses along her ribcage. 'Surely you realise that? From the moment I answered my door and found you standing there glaring at me.'

'No. . .' With no clear idea of what she was denying, Gina almost sobbed the word.

'*Ja, min kaere.*' The cultured voice had lost its clear edge, become slurred as it reverted to its mother tongue. 'And every time since then when I have kissed you, that "anything" has grown intense. . .become "something". . .'

'Twice,' Gina whispered. 'Only twice!' As if the rarity of their mouths meeting could negate his claim. Once in anger in this apartment, once more in Ib's Club to irritate Lotta. . .

'Three times,' he corrected softly, claiming her mouth, which opened to him without protest as her body went limp. Now the doubts in her mind were obliterated as a searing excitement took over, leaving her with no thought of evasion, no thought of anything but to respond completely, to enjoy the strength and purpose, the seductive presence of Rune Christensen, filling her senses with him, tasting, touching. . . enjoying. . .

She was melting, dissolving into a stream of molten need, every nerve-end sensitised and throbbing for requitement.

'Rune. . .' She made one last feeble attempt to avoid the escalation of physical craving between them, knowing she had lost when she heard the unusual huskiness of her own voice, and saw Rune's eyes darken in immediate response.

'Hush, *mus*.' His fingers laced in her hair, as his thumbs traced the delicate lines of her temples. His voice was low and deep, vibrant with a hard-held patience, as if he already sensed the latent protest in the way she'd breathed his name. He was holding her there without duress, pinning her where she sat by the sheer magnetism of his physical presence.

Now was the time to say no, to deny him while the pressured timbre of his voice still echoed in her mind, threatening whatever barriers had withstood his onslaught to date.

'Rune. . .' His name trembled on her lips once more, no longer a name but an endearment, a paean to the deep spring of emotion which was gushing through her, banishing logical thought, obliterating words like 'giving' and 'taking', replacing them with 'sharing'. She had stopped thinking—now there was only feeling. . .

Lifting her with effortless strength to her feet, he cradled her against the hard strength of his own body. The repeated touch of his mouth on her own thrilled through her, tasting her with such erotic intensity that she gasped, straining against him, seeking the solace of his flesh, assuaging the ache in her own trembling limbs by pressing herself against his adamant masculine frame.

Moaning softly, she found herself totally unable to control her unfettered response. Like a dam bursting, her feelings overwhelmed her with their sudden surge. At last she could admit honestly to herself that some part of her had been waiting all evening for this moment when her own self-imposed barriers would be swept away.

Images flickered across the disordered screen of her mind—Rune provocatively, dominantly angry at their first meeting; Rune, eyes shuttered, playing 'her' song; Rune, mouth tender, eyes laughing as he had watched the children playing at the funfair in Tivoli; Rune, seeking her out at her hotel, deliberately drawing her into his life; Rune, his blond head bent, handling her damaged foot with such tenderness; Rune. . .

She moaned softly, returning his kisses, sliding her

hands up and down his back, glorying in his unrestrained response as he shuddered at her exploratory touch.

She was drowning in sensory pleasure as his mouth moved from hers to place its erotic touch on her eyelids, her temples, followed the high line of her sculptured cheekbone, every movement speaking of his possessive need, his mounting passion, his overriding desire to invade and conquer her. As his firm, predatory fingers stroked her body, following her soft curves with a barely restrained urgency, she wondered if it would be enough for either of them if she were to withdraw now from their headlong fall into physical ecstasy.

Drowsily, achingly she allowed him to explore her flesh where it was revealed above the neckline of her pretty dress. Suddenly it was no longer enough to accept his caresses without responding. Her fingers itched to feel his silken flesh beneath them, memories of their first meeting taunting her as she pulled at his shirt, easing it from his trousers. Deep in her subconscious mind the image of Lotta became one-dimensional, faded, crumpled, ceased to exist.

Rune's whole body shivered as her cool palms moved spasmodically over his heated flesh. Smooth as oiled silk, his skin excited her delicate touch. She allowed her fingers to roam, her eyes tightly shut, her mind vividly picturing him as she had seen him for the very first time. Tuesday—could it really be only Tuesday when now every cell of her body was alight with a feedback intelligence that told her she had been waiting for this man all her life. . .

Rune was fuelling her fantasies, playing a descant to her theme, somehow sensing her rhythm, exciting and tormenting her. She was unbearably aware of the tensile strength of his incipient beard beneath the shaven smoothness of his jaw, just as she was of the aroused hardness of his body, controlled, contained but testifying to his rampant masculinity in a way that was driving her to abandon the last remaining threads of self-control.

It was the sound of a dull thud from the direction of the bedroom which brought her down to earth with shattering finality, icing her blood, freezing her to the spot. No! Not again! Dear God—not the same scenario of shame and perversion!

'I have to go!' Fear thawed her, lending her unusual strength as she tore herself out of Rune's arms, desire draining from her body and leaving her cold and shaken.

'Gina! No, wait!' Rune barred her way, staring down at her with puzzled, angry eyes, his breath sawing heavily between his teeth. 'What's wrong?'

'You! You're what's wrong!' She was shouting now, scorching with pain, pushing at his hard chest in a futile effort to move him away from the door. 'I hate you! I want to go back to my hotel.'

'Yes, yes, all right. Of course you shall go back, but not before you tell me what's upset you,' he retorted roughly. 'Look, I can take rejection as well as the next man, perhaps even better! What I can't take is seeing you distressed like this and not knowing why. A few moments ago I could swear that you didn't hate me.' His eyes darkened with some unknown emotion. 'Did you think I was going to rape you?'

'I don't owe you anything. . .' Tears were building up behind her eyes, threatening to disgrace her by spilling down her cheeks. She who had long since learned the necessary control to hide her feelings was about to suffer the greatest humiliation of all, the fall of angry tears which would betray her sensitivity, leaving her naked and vulnerable before this man whom she had begun to trust. . .and his friends. . .

Through the mists of her muddled thinking came the name which had wounded her and could now save her.

'Marcus. . .' She spoke it from between trembling lips like a sob.

'The man you're waiting for to make you his wife?' Rune glared at her with savage eyes. 'Even if I'd believed that story when you told it to me, I certainly wouldn't believe it now. Not after what has just happened between us.'

'Nothing has happened,' she whispered, raising her hands to her bare arms, trying to soothe the goose-pimples which marred their smooth surface. 'Nothing that can't be written off as a momentary aberration between a man and a woman. Please just let me go. I'm sorry if I let you think I wanted to. . .'

'Make love with me?' He finished her sentence, blue eyes sweeping over her thoughtfully. 'Something frightened you, *min skat*, but it wasn't me, was it? And it wasn't because you suddenly remembered you were in love with another man, because you're not the kind of girl who plays away from home. Believe me, I can tell!'

At any other time she would have recognised the bitter note of personal experience in his voice, but all she wanted at that moment was to flee before her worst fears were realised.

'Rune, please. . .' Desperately she pleaded but to no avail.

'But this guy, this Marcus has something to do with what you are feeling now. . .fear? Disgust?'

'I don't want to talk about it!' She was beginning to shake. 'You're right. I don't play away from home. I don't play games at all! Any games at all—do you understand?'

Temper came to her aid, flushing her waxen cheeks

with rose, causing her breasts to rise and fall in agitation. 'So you can tell your friends they can stop hiding and smirking. The cabaret is going home!'

It was as if she had shot him with a tranquillising dart. Rune froze where he stood, a look of total incomprehension on his face.

'I heard the noise. . .' She was controlling her voice with enormous effort. 'In your bedroom. I'm not as naïve as I may seem.'

'You think there is someone in there?' He stared at her, brows furrowed, as if she were mad.

'One, two, maybe more—how would I know?' She made a valiant attempt to shrug her shoulders, succeeding only in displaying a deep shudder.

'*Du gode Gud!*' He moved with incredible speed, seizing her by the shoulders and propelling her towards the closed door, a hard violence etching the bones of his face into a mask that would have just done justice to a Viking warrior at his most rapacious.

'Rune—no!' Unable to prevent his speedy passage, she screwed her eyes up tightly, her body rigid in his hands as he flung the door open. She had expected raucous laughter, giggling, cries of disappointment— anything but the total silence that struck her eardrums with the cold effectiveness of a block of ice applied to her nervous system.

'Open your eyes, Gina—see for yourself.' His hands which had clasped her so tightly eased their pressure, holding her now with the gentle touch of a friend.

'Obediently she did as he bade her, her gaze travelling round the empty room, seeing only the elegant lines of fitted furniture, the newly made bed, the bedside table with one large volume hanging open— and another fallen untidily on the floor beside it. Obviously their combined weight had overbalanced them.

'So, is that what your Marcus did?' Rune's hands moved soothingly on the cool flesh of her arms, demanding her confidence. 'Trapped you into playing a part in an orgy?'

'We'd been going out together on dates for a month or so,' she began haltingly, too emotionally drained to refuse him the information he wanted. 'He was very attractive, very attentive. . .he wasn't like the other men I knew. He seemed to like me as a person—I felt I could trust him.' She laughed bitterly, pausing before continuing, her voice becoming firmer, assured by Rune's sensitive silence. 'This particular evening we'd been to see the latest Lloyd Webber musical and I was high on the music, treading on air. . .'

Why was she telling him this, reliving her humiliation for his vicarious enjoyment? Only Rune wasn't amused. His face was still, his mouth held in a taut beautiful line, his eyes as cold as an arctic glacier as he encouraged her to continue with the slightest nod of his head.

'We went back to his flat.' She moved her shoulders in a hopeless gesture of defeat. 'I'd convinced myself I loved him. . .that he loved me. . .' She shook her head despairingly at the girl she had once been. Cinderella expecting celestial fulfilment with the handsome prince. . .'It was only when the doorbell rang and two more couples joined us that I realised what he had in mind.' She had been stunned, shocked, hurt beyond belief. Perhaps Marcus had read her previous reticence to give herself completely to him as boredom with the scenario of casual individual relationships which were par for the course for their contemporaries, and had laid on a partner-swapping party to titillate her interest.

'He's in merchant banking,' she whispered. 'He seemed so solid, reliable. I thought he was being considerate with me, not rushing me. I didn't realise that his tastes were more esoteric. I felt so green, so hurt—so humiliated.'

'My poor *mus*.' Behind the mocking intonation of Rune's deep voice was a glimmer of tenderness. 'He didn't know the first thing about you, did he?'

Wearily she shook her head. Didn't know and hadn't wanted to! She'd fled, but not before he'd accused her with brutish, angry words of a number of character and personality deficiencies, the greatest of which appeared to be her total inability to appreciate the finer qualities of Marcus Pritchard.

CHAPTER NINE

'AH, GINA . . .how could you compare me with an insensitive brute like that?' The calm sympathy of Rune's voice acted like a balm on her tortured nerves. 'Haven't you realised yet how selfish I am with the things I own, protecting them, defending them?'

'I'm not a thing, not a work of art to be cherished and admired, a creation whose value will only increase with time,' she whispered, wishing she could find the strength to walk away from him, but feeling herself trapped by the powerful presence of his closeness, the warmth of his body, the erotic aura of his total maleness, a strength of spirit which went beyond the mere physical. Mad though it was, at that moment she wanted to be a part of him. Wanted to feed on his masculine dominance, to take his vibrant power with the lure of her own body, to please and be pleasured by him and then to flee, to make her escape back to England without recrimination or the need to analyse her feelings. For the first time in her life she wasn't being rational, and the realisation both excited and horrified her. 'Neither do you own me,' she added breathlessly.

'No, you're not a thing.' He gathered her to him, his voice low, crooning, as soothing as honey on a wound. 'You're flesh and blood, warm and yielding, bursting into my life at a time when I'd sworn to give women a wide berth, enticing me with your large eyes and your candour, your raven hair and your loyalty. . .' He was kissing her with small caresses of his mouth, teasing her cheeks and nose, tempting her brows and the corners of her mouth, so that her breath grew shallow and her body leaned against his solid frame for support. 'But I will own you, *min søde*, because I won't rest until I do. Let me show you that all men aren't as cruel and immature as your retarded merchant banker. Give me your freshness and coolness—let me devour them with my strength and fire. . .'

His voice had deepened, the words becoming more guttural as for the first time since she'd met him he seemed to struggle with a language which was not his own. Gina gave a little cry, half-sigh, half-despair as she recognised the allusion he had made to the aquavit in Ib's Club. Even then he'd wanted her. . . But surely only as a substitute for the exquisite, capricious Lotta? Wasn't Rune Christensen as much a player of games as the man he purported to despise? Or was it possible, as he claimed, that Lotta had misrepresented the situation with calculated spite?

Somehow she couldn't find the strength to confront him with her suspicions again, and, if she had, what would he have done? Denounced them, denied them as he had already. No, better to hold her peace and pretend. Pretend that he loved her—her, Georgina Price—for what she was—shy and frigid, thin-skinned and strait-laced. She would be hurting no one because, even if Rune had lied and was still involved in some emotional way with Lotta, the Swedish girl had already assumed they were lovers and obviously accepted them in that role without suffering undue pain.

So, when Rune's English gave way to Danish once more, she made her own translation of the words, inventing the compliments and vows she wanted to hear, feeling her pulse respond more rapidly still as his voice deepened and shook with fervour.

When at last his lean fingers framed her face, tense

against her skin and his eyes silently pleaded for her acquiescence, she finally found her voice.

'Yes,' she whispered, '*Ja*, Rune.'

He lifted and carried her the few necessary steps, until she felt the yielding softness of his bed beneath her back. Lying still, drugged by her own fantasies, she watched as he shrugged off his clothes with minimum effort, a lean efficiency of movement that left him naked, muscled and golden like a god from the pages of Nordic mythology.

She welcomed him with outstretched arms as he came to her, knowing there was no retreat now and glorying in the thought of her forthcoming submission. This would be, for both of them, an expiation of emotional suffering.

By the time Rune had unclothed her completely Gina's whole body knew the intimate touch of his mouth and hands and had become a conflagration of need for the ultimate knowledge of the man himself.

Somewhere on another plane of existence she knew that he was pacing himself, tuning himself to her slower needs: that his tiny muted cries of painful frustration were evidence of his consideration as he aroused her to an aching, trembling plateau of desire.

'Now, Rune, now. . .' she pleaded when she felt her whole universe was on the point of disintegrating. Pressing her body against his, she wound her arms and legs around him, urging him to satisfy her. . .to satisfy them both.

'*Ja*', he whispered, as she caressed his corded neck with her open mouth, overwhelmed by the scent and taste of his heated, sweat-dampened skin. '*Ja, min elskede.*'

She had expected pain, almost welcomed it as the payment for ridding herself of her despised virginity which had labelled her in her own mind as undesired—

unloved. Instead there was only a blazing, triumphant surge of fulfilment as she accepted the fullness of Rune's body into her own, and a mounting sense of exhilaration as he began to move in the age-old rhythm of possession.

'Rune. . . Rune. . . Rune.' With every thrust she gasped his name like an incantation, sensing his pleasure as the syllable burst from her love-swollen mouth, turning her head on the softness of the pillow spread with the sable blackness of her hair.

'*Min mus, min elskede. . .*' His voice was laboured, a growl in his throat. '*Jeg elsker dig.*'

Every one of her senses sharpened to its utmost Gina entered a world as unreal and beautiful as Tivoli itself, mindlessly letting conscious thought give way to pure sensation, as his voice caressed her ears with words which could only be endearments, husky and broken. For the first time in her life she felt the fetters of discipline and caution falling from her as her spirit, fired by the ritual movements of her supple body, soared to another plane.

No matter that she hadn't understood the broken phrases gasped from Rune's lips as he had devoured her with his kisses; she knew instinctively that they had been an expression of his desire for her in that sweet moment of culmination. She wanted to tell him that she loved him, but they were words she had never spoken to anyone. Sacred, potent words that she couldn't bear to throw like confetti into the breeze, however bright and brilliant the climate of the moment.

Then she was crying aloud as she felt her body quickening to climax, and the tears wet on her own cheeks as she soared to a summit she had never hoped to experience, as beautiful and spectacular and as free as the fireworks of Tivoli and, like them, over too soon, leaving her both satiated yet hungry to renew the experience.

There was no need for words between them, no postmortem, as Rune relieved her of the burden of his weight, drawing her to him, pulling her dark head down on his strong golden shoulder agleam with the sparkling moisture of his sweet, clean sweat. Her body, limp now, warm and damp with the evidence of his passion, lay passively against him, filling his hard, shallow male contours with the softness of her flowing curves, as she let her senses absorb him, his taste, his touch, the scent of him, the sound of his heavy, steady breathing, and the sight of his beautiful face where at the moment of consummation passion and compassion had mingled to win her trust.

It was light when she awakened and eased her limbs to a more comfortable position on the soft bed. Beside her Rune slept like the proverbial baby, brow unfurrowed, mouth closed, lips slightly curled as if his dreams pleased him, golden brown lashes, tipped with ash-blond, an innocent sweep against the high carved Nordic cheekbones. He was like a young and virile counterpart of Holger Danske, one of Denmark's greatest mythical heroes, whom tradition decreed repelled all invaders in the early Viking age before falling into a deep sleep. Only if Denmark's freedom were ever to be threatened, so the legend ran, would he reawaken in her defence.

Strange, Gina thought, how much their two countries had in common and how little she had realised that element of kinship before. Both countries had democratic monarchies, valued their precious right to freedom of speech, enjoyed a good standard of living yet gave generously to less fortunate nations. Looking down at the face of her lover, she smiled, daring to trace the line of his profile with a tender finger. Why, England even had its own equivalent of Holger Danske in her own King Arthur, who, it was said, would rise again from his round table and with his Knights of Camelot ride to the defence of the realm he loved, should the need arise.

Rune stirred slightly but didn't awaken as Gina's wandering finger followed the hollow of his cheekbone, grazing against the blond stubble of his jaw. Tough, she thought, like the man himself. From the beginning he had been determined to bed her. In retrospect she could see that quite plainly. The old Gina, the one who had guarded her own virginity as if it had been her sole worth, would have awakened from the experience ashamed and remorseful. She sighed without regret. The new Gina had been liberated. It was one of the many things for which she had Rune to thank. Despite what had happened between them, because it had been what she had wanted at the time and because Rune had been a generous and not over-demanding lover, and because she loved him, her own sense of self-esteem had remained whole.

Because she loved him! Her hand froze against his cheek as the realisation tensed every muscle in her body. No! This way madness and disillusionment lay. Rune had never pretended an emotional attachment to her—in fact quite the opposite! Liking, let alone loving, had never been a requisite for the majority of men whose capacity for making love was triggered more by the physical attributes of a woman than the quality of her personality or character! She shivered as she recalled Lotta's beautiful, animated face. Did Rune, despite his disclaimers, feel more for Lotta than mere desire as the other girl had claimed? Did he still? The overtones of a heavy relationship had been everywhere that night at Ib's Club. Yet according to Rune the affair had ended more than six months ago.

Gina sighed. She was doing what all men hated: holding a post-mortem on an event which was no more important in the scheme of life than the enjoyment of a good wine! Yes, she was being absurd. She'd gone to bed with Rune willingly, with both eyes wide open in a metaphorical sense, knowing his background and aware that, in the natural, uncomplicated atmosphere of Scandinavia, perhaps more than anywhere else in Europe there were fewer taboos regarding physical relationships between couples. At least it was comforting to know that he wouldn't consider her compliance 'cheap' or despise her for the speed with which he had been able to seduce her.

She tried to dismiss the odd feeling of anticlimax she was experiencing. The truth was, she had a lot to be grateful for. Rune had treated her body with a considerate respect that had been faultless, ensuring her safety, even as he had ensured her ecstasy. He'd given her so much and she would never forget him, but she would never confuse what they had shared with that elusive emotion—love. One-sided, such a feeling could be more destructive than exhilarating.

'Ow!' Her silent philosophising ended with a yelp of indignation as she found her forefinger nipped between strong white teeth.

'How are you this morning, *min skat*?' he asked her gently.

'Fine!' She deliberately kept her voice casual, one heavy strand of black hair falling across her cheek as she returned his intense scrutiny.

'Good.' His clear blue eyes were amused as he pulled himself upright, looking cool and collected, his gaze moving with tender appreciation over her uncovered opaline breasts. 'I must admit I thought that in retrospect you might resent what happened between us last night.'

'Why should I?' She assumed the air of sang-froid so well known to her acquaintances back in England. 'I'm not so green that I don't know what a man means when he invites a woman back to his flat after midnight.' She was delighted by the carefree lightness of her voice as hastily she began to move to the side of the bed, inwardly quaking but determined not to reveal by the merest movement her reservations to him about revealing her total nakedness by the growing light of day as it filtered through the perpendicular blinds.

'Wait!' His arm snaked out, pinioning her round her waist, drawing her back against his body, holding her firmly so that she could feel the thunder of his heart against her back. 'I had no intention of becoming your lover last night when I invited you back here. I truly did intend to discuss business.'

'But the woman tempted me?' she suggested, her laugh a trifle forced. 'I seem to remember that excuse has already been used by the man who got the human race thrown out of Eden.'

He shook his head slowly. 'It was my fault. I thought I could handle the situation. I underestimated the effect you have on me, *mus*.'

Fault? The word sliced through her like a knife-blade, leaving a clean, smarting pain in its wake.

'You're saying you regret it?' She quivered in his grasp, trying to maintain her air of sophistication as her voice dipped unsteadily. 'I'm sorry if I disappointed you. I'd forgotten you'd already classed me and my sister as experienced *femme fatales*, luring men to their doom!'

'She-devil!' His half-smile was rueful as with deliberate intention he smoothed his palm over her taut nipples, starting a wild drumming somewhere inside her. Defensively she pushed his hand away, staring at him with dark-pupilled eyes, the clear grey irises ringed with silver. 'On the contrary, whatever I supposed your sister to be, I suspected your basic innocence from the moment we crossed the Rådhuspladsen that first night and I heard the long-drawn-out note of the *lur*.'

'That's not amusing,' she snapped. He was laughing at her inexperience, making her feel gauche and defenceless.

'Well, perhaps it was a stray note from a wayward clarinet in one of the jazz clubs,' he conceded easily. Then the humour left his face. 'No, the only thing I regret is that I may have rushed you into something you're already beginning to repent. Did I, Gina?'

'Good heavens, no!' Now he was the one determined on a post-mortem. 'In fact it was the perfect ending to a perfect evening.' Pleased with the insouciance in her carefully modulated tone, Gina gave him a polished smile. Didn't he think she was sophisticated enough not to expect commitment after a one-night stand?

'Good.' Despite his claim of satisfaction he didn't look over-pleased. 'Then neither of us has anything with which to reproach him or herself.'

'Of course not.' Gina flashed him a bright, insincere smile, wanting nothing more than to escape from his presence before she betrayed the kind of emotions which would embarrass both of them. She looked round a little desperately for something to cover her nakedness. The only thing to hand was the duvet, and her chances of seizing that away from Rune were negligible. Ah, well. Taking a deep breath, she moved with a sudden thrust, propelling herself away from his arms off the bed and on to the floor. 'My immediate plans are to have a shower and dress and then perhaps we can discuss your proposed advertising campaign?' Something in his expression halted her headlong flight

towards the en-suite bathroom. 'Or was that just a ploy
to. . .?' Her voice tailed away as with a seemingly
effortless movement he found his feet, and bounded
across the short distance to block her passage.

Oh, dear God! In the dim light of the evening he
had been magnificent. Now, naked, simmering with
annoyance, the deepening light gilding him, he was no
less imposing. Absurdly, she wanted to lay her head on
his broad, muscled chest, feel the strength of his arms
surround and protect her. She, who'd always stood on
her own feet, fought her own battles. Ashamed of the
breach he'd made in her defences, she drew on her
inner courage to confront him, tilting her chin fiercely.

'Ploy, Gina?' he growled, his ice-blue eyes intent on
her face. 'You think I can't get a woman to come to
bed with me without offering her bribes? You think I
have to pay for my pleasures?'

'No, of course not!' What had she meant? Only that
perhaps he had manufactured some reason so that she
would be able to overcome her own personal fears of
being alone with him; given her an excuse to accept his
invitation to re-enter the apartment where he'd pre-
viously abused her both physically and verbally. She
tried to find the right words to explain but discovered
only a great disconnection between her brain and her
voice, which ensured her silence. All she was capable
of doing was gazing at him, hardly aware of her own
nakedness, while her eyes and her mind told her that,
far from having to pay for women's favours, if Runo
Christensen had been so inclined he could have made
a fortune as a gigolo. But of course he wasn't so
inclined, not when women as beautiful as Lotta Pettersson were throwing themselves at his feet!

'So. . .' he breathed, strong arms seizing her bare
shoulders. 'You thought your chance of handling my
account depended on how well you handled my——'

'Rune!' Cheeks scarlet, she truncated his sentence.

'——my demands in bed,' he finished softly. 'Well, you were wrong. The two things were entirely unconnected, but if it is of importance to you then you'll be pleased to know that had there been a test you would have passed it with straight As.'

'Let me pass—please.' She tried to sidestep him, but he forestalled her movement.

'What are you running away from, Gina? What was so terrible about last night that you can't get far enough away from it? Or is it me? If you didn't think you were being blackmailed into bed, were you just looking for a man, any man, to wipe out the memory of Marcus, to prove you're a normal, beautiful, loving woman— and now you've proved that, you find you don't even *like* the man you chose to be your therapist?'

'Let me go. . .' It was little more than a whimper as she shook her head, refusing to answer. A small spurt of ironic laughter choked in her throat. Imagine his face if she told him the truth: that, far from not liking him, she was labouring under this absurd fantasy that she loved him—for how else could she explain the turmoil that heaved inside her mind and body? And how dared he try to bolster up his male ego at her expense when he had made it so plain he didn't care a damn for her as a person?

'Not before you give me your answer, *min søde* Gina,' he said softly.

'Very well.' Her brain was working quickly now, seeking a way to heal the breaches he had made in the armour of her emotional defence. 'Of course I like you, Rune. You're a very attractive man—as I'm sure you know. But last night was a one-off. We were both looking for comfort—I because of Marcus, you because of Lotta—and we found it together. That doesn't mean it has to happen again.'

'Oh, I see,' he drawled with a touch of cool insolence. 'So you *were* using me as a stud, *min kaere*. I ask you if you like me and you tell me you "fancy" me—isn't that the word you British use to describe a lustful attraction?' His eyes rested on her, alive with cool speculation. 'Well, who am I to argue with that? It will make our future association all the more interesting and rewarding.'

'Oh, this is is absurd!' They were standing as naked as Adam and Eve before the Fall, and the incongruity of her situation struck Gina with unpleasant impact. Once more she tried to elude him, but as before he was too fast for her.

'Too right it is!' he agreed, reaching for her with masterly precision and pulling her up against him, ignoring her small cry of outrage. His body was warm and hard against her own shivering flesh, his arms binding her to him as her reason spun helplessly beneath the sudden sensual onslaught.

She tried to fight him, but her effort was half-hearted as she found herself carried away on an irresistible tide of longing. There wasn't any time to repulse him either with words or actions as his seeking mouth found her tender lips. It was all there, just as it had been the previous night: the exhilaration, the mounting excitement, the warm, wonderful sensation of not being isolated and lonely.

As Rune's hard, caressing hands slid up and down her body, Gina automatically raised her arms around his neck, her fingers reaching for his hair, winding through its golden thickness, oblivious to everything save the heavy clamouring of her heart, the new-found responses of her senses to Rune's compelling masculine power.

If he'd picked her up and laid her on the bed and taken her with all the passion and strength his virile body was promising her at that moment, she wouldn't have raised a finger to stop him, so when he swung her around in his arms and deposited her nearer to the bathroom door before removing his arms from her she was left gasping with surprise and a sinking feeling of disappointment mixed with humiliation which shook her with its intensity.

'There are several things you should know about me, *min kaere* Gina,' he told her softly. 'I'm no stud, to be used to settle a score against another man, and my brain is above rather than below my belt, despite any present evidence to the contrary!' He allowed himself a small, tight smile as she clenched her teeth and remained staring him full in the face, determined not to give him the satisfaction of accepting his subtle invitation to check his statement. She knew precisely to what evidence he referred, had already experienced tactile proof of his arousal when he had held her so close to his warm naked body. So he could control his baser instincts! Good! She hoped he found the practice uncomfortable!

'Neither,' he continued in the same gentle tone of voice, 'am I prepared to be cast as some Viking lover straight out of a Hollywood film, rampaging and raping so that you can put the full responsibilities of your actions on me. Is that clear, *min skat*?'

'Perfectly.' She was already flushed with frustration and embarrassment; now her skin tingled as anger flooded her system with adrenalin.

'Good.' He nodded. 'And, while I appreciate your charitable intent in trying to comfort me for Lotta's absence from my bed, I tell you once more that the time when I might have needed consolation for Lotta's tricks has long since passed, and the fact that I've chosen to live the life of a monk for the past six months is because until the past few days I have felt no desire to give in to the temptations paraded before me.'

Did she detect a double-edged sword in that remark? A suggestion that she had consciously paraded temptation before him?

'I've always admired asceticism in a man,' she returned demurely. 'Unfortunately, in my experience it's seldom of long duration.'

'What experience, *min skat*?' he enquired sweetly.

'That of observing the merry-go-round of changing partners among my acquaintances!' she shot back, determined not to be defeated in this exchange of niceties.

'Ah!' He regarded her with calculated interest. 'Perhaps you believe that I too have ridden that carousel to excess?'

'I haven't given the matter any thought.' Airily she dismissed any curiosity about his past.

'Good. Because I have little patience for people who waste their time on idle speculation without any evidence to support their suspicions—and now,' he continued inexorably, 'since we understand each other, I suggest you go and have your shower, get dressed and eat some breakfast. Take your time—I awakened a couple of hours ago and have already attended to my own needs. Then, of course, as you so rightly mentioned, there's the matter of my air-conditioning unit,' he continued smoothly, taking a few steps away from her to slide open the door of the large built-in wardrobe to produce a maroon silk dressing-gown, which he gravely handed over to her, before finding a similar garment, this time in striped towelling, for himself.

Gratefully Gina covered her nakedness, marvelling at the strange circumstances in which she found herself. Clear-headed, efficient Gina Price—reduced to a tool in the hands of this extraordinary manipulator.

'I do feel,' Rune was continuing with the same reasonable approach with which he doubtless addressed a board meeting, 'that we need an in-depth discussion about its capabilities and design before we consider the best way to market it in the United Kingdom.'

At last she was being dismissed from his dangerous presence. Too confused to argue, she contented herself with a nod, greatly relieved when he stood aside, no longer impeding her route to the bathroom. Once inside, she slid the bolt, leaning thankfully against the door, a maelstrom of emotions fighting for supremacy. What did she really want? Half of her couldn't wait to escape from him, to relegate him to a past memory, enjoyable at the time but without consequence—like Tivoli. . .a temporary pleasuring of the senses but insubstantial. . .and the other half? The other half, she admitted to herself, wanted nothing more than to fling herself into his arms, use all her feminine wiles to attack and conquer his patronising self-control. To take what he could offer her, to lose her senses in his sweet expertise, to fool herself that, despite all the evidence to the contrary, he loved her!

She bit her lip, caught between natural caution and an untypical desire to live dangerously.

CHAPTER TEN

BY THE time she'd showered, dressed and brushed the tangles out of her hair, Gina had made her decision. Staying on in Denmark could only bring her further pain in the long run. She'd been hopelessly optimistic in supposing she could track Suzie down in the street. Despite the odds against her, she would have persevered if that had been the only hope of tracing her sister.

Now that Rune had taken charge of the whole operation, bringing in 'back-up' troops, her own futile efforts were being shown up for the amateur plan they were! Not that she intended to wipe her hands of Suzie. If her young sister needed her help, advice or support she would return instantly—a situation even more tenable since Sebastian Grantham's generous offer to settle her present flight bills!

She grimaced at her reflection in the mirror. Irritating though it was to admit it, there was little doubt that Rune Christensen's ability to handle the whole situation between Svend and Suzie would be superior to her own. She herself cared too deeply for Suzie, would be too easily swayed by the younger girl's pleas, too affected by her tears to remain impartial to her suffering. If Suzie was defiant, then she, Gina, would be torn between wanting to make both her sister and Margaret happy. Neither would she be able to disregard the disappointment of Svend's parents. Rune, on the other hand, would have no doubts as to what was best for everyone concerned. With Svend he would be tough— even brutal; with Suzie cold and implacable. She shivered. When Rune had finished with her, Suzie would want nothing better than to return hotfoot to receive Margaret's tearful forgiveness!

Thoroughly adding an extra touch of colour to her lips, Gina regarded her face contemplatively in the mirror. Prolonged contact with Rune could only make her parting from him more painful, the recovery period afterwards more protracted, the absolute cure less certain. Hopefully he would be able to tell her all she needed to know about his air-conditioning unit in a couple of hours. Armed with illustrations, specifications and his own ideas about his target market, plus knowledge of any built-in prejudices he had about the kind of media he preferred—TV, newspapers, posters, et cetera—plus of course the size of the budget he was prepared to allocate, she would be able to report with the least possible delay to Sebastian Grantham. With a bit of luck she might even get a place on a flight that very day.

The tantalising smell of coffee met her as she emerged into the main sitting-room, to see that the low table before one of the chesterfields now bore a white china breakfast-set complete with coffee-pot and plates containing rolls and Danish pastries, while a crystal jar containing some kind of preserve rested on yet another plate containing foil-covered squares of butter.

Rune, now fully dressed in casually cut light blue trousers and a navy cotton-knit shirt stretched snugly over his well-developed shoulders, was standing with his back to her, contemplating the Knudsen.

'Admiring your treasure?' she enquired lightly as he turned at her entrance.

'Every time I look at it I see some detail for the first time—a tiny insect on a stone, a bird half hidden by foliage, a shadow which yesterday escaped me. I sometimes think I may live with it for a lifetime and never really know it intimately. That each morning, like a beautiful woman, it will reveal some hidden facet to me so that I will never be bored with its presence.' He moved towards the table, indicating she join him.

Smiling politely, Gina seated herself, seizing the chance to continue talking about art. Since they were in agreement about Knudsen's work, it would be a safe subject for discussion while they ate. Anything to avoid further reference to what had happened between them the previous evening!

'No wonder you were determined to keep possession of it,' she remarked, nodding her head in thanks for the cup of black coffee he passed to her. 'Tell me, how would you describe the style—surrealistic?'

'Experts refer to it as the post-modernistic simulacrum, although I believe Knudsen himself thinks of it as fantasy realism,' he returned blandly. 'Still, as Shakespeare's Juliet said—"A rose by any other name. . ."'

'I see you're an admirer of the Bard.' Gina bit into an apricot and nut Danish pastry, acknowledging an untypical craving for sweetness, beginning to relax now the conversation had been established as impersonal.

'Of course.' Rune's blond head dipped affirmatively. 'Think how much our tourist industry is in debt to him. Every year people come from all over the World to see Kronborg castle at Helsingør because it's supposed to be the famous Elsinore where Hamlet met his doom.' He paused to take a long draught of his own coffee. 'This morning I'm taking you up the coast to my house overlooking the Sound, and if the weather stays as good as it is at the moment we'll spend the afternoon on the beach at Hornbaek, which means we'll go right past Kronberg—we can even stop off and take the tour if it appeals to you.'

'No!' Panic-stricken, Gina jumped to her feet. 'That

won't be possible. I—I've decided that since you've got everything under control there's no point in my staying here any longer. I'm going to try to get a seat on a flight to London this afternoon.'

'I see.' Lounging back where he sat, Rune stretched out his long legs, his face devoid of expression as his eyes dwelt consideringly on her agitated face.

'Yes, well. . .' His very silence drove her to further explanation. 'As I said, it can't be long before you locate Suzie, and I'm sure you'll have more success in persuading her to go home than I would.' She gave a brittle laugh. 'Suzie's always been more amenable to advice from men than she has from her own sex. Probably because she never had a father at home to look up to——' She broke off, biting her lip, knowing she was saying too much and ashamed at her loquacity. 'Anyway,' she continued bravely, staring down at her own feet as she found herself unable to meet Rune's cool appraisal, 'the fact is, I really can't afford to stay away from work for too long—from a career point of view, that is——'

'No, Gina.' His voice, dark, determined but devoid of anger, cut across her explanation.

'No—what?' Damn her own voice for shaking, but she had known this was never going to be easy.

'No, you can't go back to England today.' There was an almost imperceptible pause as she gathered her breath to argue, then he added softly, 'Not, that is, if you want to take my business with you.'

There was no hint of compassion or understanding in those beautiful blue eyes, no hint that he would even consider an appeal, but for Grantham and Marsh's sake she had to make one.

'I thought if you gave me all the details. . .' She looked wildly around her. 'You must have some specifications here, photographs——'

He shook his head. 'No. Everything you need is either at the office or at my other house. Besides, I have the system installed and working there as well, so you will have first-hand invaluable knowledge of what it looks like and how efficient it is. I thought we could have lunch in the garden after your inspection—I've already arranged for the fridge to be restocked—and afterwards, if you don't fancy going to the beach, we could go out in my boat, or I'll take you for a tour of North Zealand, through the quaint old villages with their farmhouses and gardens full of hollyhocks and the beech woods. I can show you castles and palaces——'

'Stop it!' Hands tightly clenched, Gina broke into the slow, seductive future he was forecasting for them. Hidden in his catalogue of explicit delights was the one implicit one he had carefully avoided—the one alternative she had vowed never to consider again. They could make love. Once more they could reveal themselves to each other—not just physically, because with every gesture she made she knew she would reveal the one thing he must never know—the fact that she loved him.

She swallowed deeply, wondering just how far he would go in order to try to force her to comply with his will. It seemed he held all the cards—there were other agencies who could handle his business, and if he denied Grantham and Marsh the opportunity because of her stubbornness how could she explain it to Sebastian? It would be difficult, she acknowledged. It wasn't unusual for human flesh to be the bait in an industry where million-pound budgets were on offer. On the other hand, although Sebastian Grantham might not understand her reluctance, he would respect it. Sexual favours willingly granted for profit were one thing—sexual harassment quite another.

The silence was oppressive. Rune, having obeyed her command, was sitting motionless, contenting himself by regarding her steadily through half-closed eyes. Obviously it was she who must speak first.

'My decision stands,' she told him steadily. 'For personal reasons I prefer not to spend another night here in Denmark. As far as your proposed advertising campaign is concerned, I can assure you that we will be quite capable of working from the material you supply us with, should you decide to offer us your business. If you can't obtain it from your office in time, then surely it can be sent through the post?' She had been addressing her half-eaten Danish pastry, unable to meet his penetrating eyes as she delivered her little speech. Now it was drawing to its end she gathered the courage to look him straight in the face. 'I don't wish to appear ungrateful or offensive but I have a job to get back to——'

'No, *min kaere*, Gina. I'm afraid that's another mistake you've just made. Unless you return to the UK with my business, not only do you not have a job, but the whole future of Grantham and Marsh is on the line.'

Leisurely he uncurled his large but graceful frame to stand towering over her. Instinctively she took a step away from him, her senses reeling as she felt the blood drain away from her face, and heard the buzzing in her ears which forewarned her that she was near to fainting.

'You must have guessed how precarious their balance sheet was?' Dimly his voice reached her as she drew in deep breaths of air. 'Gina, are you all right?' She heard the added urgency in his tone, felt his hands seize her shoulders, supporting her. 'Here, sit down. . .'

'No, it's all right. It was just the shock of what you

said. Yes, I did know business was bad,' she confessed. 'It was the worst possible time to be away from the office, but ——'

'You put your family first,' he finished grimly, then gave an exasperated sigh. 'There was nothing you could have done, anyway. When I made enquiries about Grantham and Marsh the whole industry was buzzing with the news that Norton Industries had just decided to move their account. It was an open secret that unless they found some other client of similar credibility and budget appropriation they couldn't continue in business.'

'No wonder Sebastian welcomed you with open arms.' She gave a bitter laugh. 'Why, Rune, why? Or were you just stringing him along for the fun of it?'

She felt his fingers tighten on her flesh as the anger in his voice seared across her consciousness. 'I don't string people along. Within two hours I had all the information I needed to know. Not only the names of their other clients but details of the campaigns, faxes of advertisements, samples of media containing some of their work. Enough to be impressed. They might not be big, but they are good. They have a certain vibrancy, an eye-catching quality, and they go for impact without forsaking good taste. If they can get a foothold in Europe they will have the chance to be bigger and better. It's as simple as that.'

'But it's not a foregone conclusion that they'll get your business?'

'Of course not,' he confirmed steadily. 'I'm a businessman, not a charity, and I'm not easy to please. But I am fair, and I appreciate quality and style when I see it.'

'It's all right—I'm not going to pass out now.' Gina gave an awkward laugh as she detached herself from his hold. It would still be touch and go for the agency.

One couldn't just get a campaign up and running overnight—although the recession bit both ways, so at least there would be space available in the media for short-term bookings. She thought of the agency folding, of having to give up her flat, of Sebastian, who had devoted his life to his business, paying with divorce as the price of his involvement, of Jenny in Media Research who had just got married and was struggling with a mortgage, or Ben, one of the account executives, whose wife was in hospital awaiting a kidney transplant. How could she let these people down because she was too afraid to face up to her own weaknesses? One client couldn't save them, but Rune's account would attract interest, give them that extra edge which would be vital in attracting others. Even the knowledge that they'd been invited to submit ideas would be like a shot of adrenalin.

'What you're saying is that unless I postpone my return to England Grantham and Marsh don't stand an iceberg's chance in hell of getting your account?' she asked baldly.

Rune sighed. 'What I'm saying is that unless you take the opportunity to see the system installed and working you'll be missing the chance of increasing your knowledge of the product and thereby depriving yourself of valuable information. To my mind practical experience outweighs textbook instruction every time.'

'I see.' On the surface it seemed a reasonable explanation. The irony was that in normal circumstances she would have insisted on seeing a working installation of a new product if only to satisfy herself that whatever she wrote wouldn't infringe the Trades Descriptions Act.

On unsteady legs she walked towards the painting, seeing for the first time the mischievous face of a gremlin peeping out beneath the skirt of an old lady bent double, sweeping a woodland path. Behind her Rune remained silent, his presence oppressive as if he were some Superman radiating a special kind of beam which could put the world to rights if only one believed in it. The strange relationship she had with him was like the painting, she thought—nothing quite what it appeared, unveiling new facets each time she considered it. Although it appeared she had a choice in making her decision, in fact she had none. What was more, Rune was perfectly aware of that fact. Her mind made up, she turned.

'What time do you want to leave for the coast?' she asked steadily.

'You are surprised at our Riviera? It isn't quite what you expected?' They had been driving northwards from Copenhagen for half an hour along the beach road when Rune posed the question.

Well, she'd truly burned her boats now, Gina had been thinking as she gazed silently out of the Mercedes's window at the passing scenery. They'd left Rune's apartment almost immediately after breakfast. He'd driven her directly to her hotel so she could change her clothes and she'd elected to wear light-weight cream cotton jeans topped by a matching sleeveless cotton stretch top, taking the precaution of carrying a jacket when Rune warned her that the breeze from the Baltic could be stiff despite the increasing warmth of the day.

He's been right about Sebastian contacting her. As soon as she'd entered the hotel she'd been handed a white envelope containing a fax message. It had been brief but positive. 'This could be our salvation,' Sebastian had written. 'Go for it—and charge all expenses to me. If you get the account we can afford them—if you don't, it won't matter anyway!'

Rune's pleasant voice penetrated her thoughts, bringing her back to the present with a small start.

'No, it isn't,' she admitted with a self-deprecatory smile, glad to keep the conversation impersonal. 'I hadn't expected anything quite so uncommercialised and natural as a string of tiny "once-upon-a-time" fishing villages and small harbours full of yachts. Its very peaceful. Everything seems so uncrowded.'

'That's because the population of Denmark is a little over five million people and it has a coastline of nearly five thousand miles, so even in the tourist season our beaches don't get packed!'

Did she detect a certain smugness in his tone? A sense of mischief forced her to challenge it.

'The water doesn't look very warm!'

The two-lane road was winding its way sometimes so close to the sparkling sea that Gina felt she could lean out of the window and dabble her hand in it. Occasionally it turned a little inland to pass through beech forests, leaving large tracts of green, wooded land bounding on to the sea. Through the trees she could sometimes see the roofs of houses. The beach here was narrow and unpopulated, although there were plenty of small yachts out on the water.

'More bracing than warm, perhaps,' Rune conceded. 'But we enjoy it. Later you shall try it for yourself.'

'Sorry, but I didn't pack a swimsuit,' she disillusioned him swiftly. 'I had no intention of spending time on a beach when I left London.'

His quick sideways glance absorbed her neat outfit speculatively.

'That's no problem. It's quite permissible here, in fact quite normal, not to bother with wearing one. We Danes get so little sun that when it does shine on us we like to take full advantage of it.'

'Fine!' She shot him a cool glance. 'You might be

prepared to make an exhibition of yourself, but I'm afraid I'm not so uninhibited. Do you mean to tell me that people actually walk about naked on all the beaches and no one complains?'

He shrugged. 'Nudity certainly isn't obligatory; it's a matter of choice, and just as many people choose to cover themselves as not. It's just that, unlike some other European countries, nakedness on a beach isn't considered a crime. Although I must admit. . .' he paused to slow the car down before turning off the road to come to a halt outside an attractive inn, thatched, gabled and wooden-beamed, its façade ablaze with baskets of flowers, its forecourt furnished with long trestle-tables and carved wooden chairs. '. . .we do get a few complaints—generally from male tourists whose culture is much more restrictive than ours, and who have mistakenly assumed that when a young woman displays herself naked on a beach she is inviting their carnal attentions. I'm afraid they feel rather frustrated when it is made clear to them that this is far from the case,' he added drily.

On the point of commenting scathingly that not everyone could be expected to be as cold-blooded as he was, Gina hesitated, finally deciding that in this case discretion was certainly the better part of valour. Rune had already demonstrated to her that he was far from cold-blooded. Controlled, perhaps, but never cold. For hadn't she already experienced the heat of the fires which burned beneath his deceptively cool surface? The last thing she wanted to do was to encourage their flaring in response to an incautious comment, especially as, since he had got his own way about her not flying out that day, his behaviour had been impeccable.

So she held her tongue as he alighted and went round to open the passenger door, offering her his hand.

'This is one of the old coaching inns. I thought you might like to stop for a coffee.'

'That would be lovely.' She accepted his gesture of courtesy, the touch of his hand sending an unexpected thrill shooting through her system. Static electricity— that was the only explanation—although from his bland expression he had felt no similar spark on contact.

With a cup of delicious coffee before her, Gina lifted her face towards the cloudless sky, enjoying the cool breeze which lifted the hair from her temples. Strange, she had been in Denmark for so short a time yet in those few days she had learned so much, not only about herself but about a country she had never even considered visiting before Suzie's escapade. She should be blessing her young sister rather than cursing her, she thought wryly.

'You obviously approve of the Whisky Belt?' Rune's soft voice interrupted her reverie.

'Whisky Belt?' Her dark eyebrows lifted questioningly.

'The colloquial name for this part of the coast because it's where some of our more wealthy citizens live,' he explained, his eyes bright with amusement. 'There's a high levy on alcohol, you see, so it's considered a luxury product.'

'I suppose the British equivalent would be what we call the Stockbroker Belt,' she mused, 'although some of those have fared pretty badly recently. You know I have to admit my knowledge of your country is abysmally small—but the more I see of it, the more I find myself falling in love with it.'

'Is that so?' Rune's eyes gleamed with pleasure as she detected an added warmth in the timbre of his voice. 'We think it's pretty special ourselves—the land of beech trees, storks and marguerites—and you've only seen such a small part of it. Wait until I've shown you the fabulous coast of Jutland and taken you to the island of Fyn where I was born. I swear I shall make you lose your heart completely!'

Quickly Gina glanced away, unable to meet the sparkling magnetism of his eyes with any pretence of equanimity. Had he guessed how she felt about him? No, there was no double meaning in what he'd said. He had no idea that their casual coupling had lit such passionate fires in her heart.

Despite the warmth of the day, she shivered. How could she have ever fallen for Marcus's attractive looks and been blind to the shallowness of his character? Because the signs had been there all the time if she'd ever bothered to look further than his surface charm.

Rune was made of sterner stuff, possessing an iron will and sense of purpose and duty that in comparison left Marcus's attitude to life looking lightweight and immature. Not that Rune couldn't be charming when he wanted to, she reflected. But she'd also seen other facets of his character, knew it to be deep and complex. In his own way he was as dangerous as Marcus—hadn't he already trapped her into staying with him longer than she deemed either necessary or wise? And now he was insinuating that she would be extending her stay long enough for a tour of the whole country! What satisfaction was he getting from this subtle form of blackmail? Or was he just trying to provoke her into an argument for the sheer hell of it? Well, she'd ignore his pointed remark. Unfortunately her determination didn't prevent a slight shiver of apprehension traversing her nervous system.

'Cold?' He'd seen her shudder and was rising to his feet, his gaze resting momentarily on her breasts, making her self-consciously aware of the thrust of her nipples against the stretch fabric. 'We'd better get back in the car. It's a little breezy here.'

She accepted his diagnosis without comment, following him back, content to sit beside him as they continued on their way through the pleasant countryside. After a few moments of silence he pressed the button of an integral cassette-player beneath the dashboard and she was delighted to hear the opening bars of Mendelssohn's Third Symphony.

'Will the music annoy you?' he asked politely.

She shook her head. 'The Scottish Symphony is one of my favourites,' she told him honestly. 'And somehow it seems to fit in with this landscape too—perhaps it's the sense of space. . .'

'Perhaps,' he agreed before lapsing into silence, but not before she'd seen his face reflect the pleasure he'd experienced at her instant recognition of what was clearly one of his favourite recordings.

'Well, we've arrived!'

She'd been so immersed in the music, letting it wash over her, uplifting her, that she hadn't even realised that the car had turned into a short driveway to stop outside a luxurious chalet-type building set in a clearing of beech trees.

Following him through the double front door, she received an instant impression of coolness and light; polished wooden floors strewn with traditional rugs, simple clean-lined furniture in the Danish tradition and pastel-coloured walls. Large double-glazed doors offered a vista of lawn and, beyond, a narrow shingle beach with a short jetty to which a small sailing boat was tied.

'It's beautiful.' Feeling Rune's eyes on her, she turned enthusiastically towards him, making no attempt to hide her ingenuous pleasure. It was then that she noticed the slightly deeper-coloured patch on the wall behind him. Instantly she knew what had caused it. It was where the Knudsen had once hung. How stupid she'd been not to realise it from the start.

Rune had brought her to the home he'd shared with Lotta for—how long? Two years, the Swedish girl had said. According to Lotta it had been Rune who had stormed out, taking the painting with him, which meant what? That any moment there would be the sound of footsteps on the stairs and the beautiful blonde would arrive to welcome her recalcitrant lover back into her life? Had she fallen yet again for his tricks? Allowed herself to be the meat in the sandwich or, more aptly perhaps, in the circumstances, the butter on the *smørrebrød*?

All her insecurities surged painfully as, throwing caution to the winds, she confronted him furiously, demanding imperiously, 'Why exactly have you brought me here, Rune? To see your fabulous new system—or to provoke your fabulous live-in lover?'

CHAPTER ELEVEN

'YOU mean Lotta Pettersson?' He aped innocent surprise, blue eyes widening in simulated astonishment.

'You have another live-in lover?' Gina asked tightly.

'You find the possibility disturbing?' He was deliberately trying to antagonise her, but behind his innocent stare she could feel a growing tension in the atmosphere.

'The only thing which disturbs me is if you brought me down here on false pretenses. I came here to see the installation of an air-conditioning unit, not to be involved in your personal life!'

'And the one necessarily precludes the other in your estimation, hmm?' The look he slanted her was quizzical, almost as if he was humouring her. 'Have you never heard of mixing business with pleasure?'

'Too often to accept the premise with any degree of equanimity,' Gina returned drily. 'In my experience such arrangements usually end in tears for at least one of the protagonists.'

Laughter gleamed in his eyes as he met her belligerent stare. 'Then you'll doubtless be delighted to learn that I haven't cried since the day I decided to go boating on the duck pond at home, only to find when I was halfway across that my rowing-boat was holed. As I was only three at the time, I lacked confidence in my ability to make it back to dry land under my own steam.'

'Obviously you underestimated your own prowess.' Despite her anxiety about his present intentions, Gina couldn't resist teasing him by casting appraising eyes over his well-muscled form.

He shook his head. 'No. I underestimated Hanne's conscientiousness in keeping an eye on me. I might have escaped her vigilence when I made off with the boat, but my wails of distress soon brought her running to the rescue. Fortunately the pond is only three feet deep at the most, so the rescue didn't overtax her capabilities.'

'Shame on you.' Gina regarded his smug expression with barely disguised amusement. 'I hope you were made to pay the penalty for your rashness!'

'If by that remark you mean you hope I was thrashed within an inch of my life, then I have to disappoint you. Here in Denmark it is not the done thing for parents to strike their children.' He contemplated her from beneath lowered eyelids, his head tilted a little to one side, summing her up as though her mind was an open book to him. 'Do I detect a desire for retribution against me, sweet Gina?'

He was reading her too well, despite her attempt to disguise her feelings. The frustration of what she could only identify as love for him, plus the fact that she'd given herself to him so completely, mixed with her suspicion that he was still using her in some way to further his own undisclosed purposes, had engendered a turmoil of emotions within her, among which, she was ashamed and horrified to realise, lurked a certain impulse to exercise violence on his person.

Banishing any such idea from her mind, she forced herself to assume an air of detachment.

'My only desire is to ensure that I remain dry-eyed,' she told him with a detachment she certainly didn't feel. 'So if your invitation to inspect your installment was genuine, could we please start?'

'Of course,' he agreed smoothly. 'And, since you

obviously assume otherwise, despite my constant reas-
surances on the subject, I'd like to take this opportunity
of assuring you that none of my liaisons—past or
present—will be lurking in the cupboards. Least of all
Lotta Pettersson. As I've already told you, there is
nothing between us except a mutual disenchantment.
She left this house at my invitation six months ago, for
good. Now, if you'll come this way, please. . .'

He took her to every room in the house and with a
cool economy of speech explained the merits of the
installation, pointing out its adaptability and demon-
strating its efficacy.

It was as if her mind had split into two separate
portions, Gina thought as with one part of it she
listened attentively to the technical explanations and
absorbed the aesthetic appearance of the system with
approving eyes, her creative instincts stimulated with
the challenge with which she'd been bestowed. But
there was another part of her brain which insisted on
presenting her with images of Lotta sharing this idyllic
environment with Rune.

Lotta cooking in the fabulous kitchen; Lotta relaxed
on the teak and leather couch of the living-room
enjoying the vista of the sea beyond the great beeches;
Lotta naked in the elegant bathroom, laughing beneath
the shower, beckoning her handsome blond lover to
join her; Lotta sprawled on the black and white striped
duvet cover of the large double bed, her shining gold
cap of hair gleaming against its darkness, her body a
pearly invitation. . .

What was it he had told her in Tivoli? 'Whatever
intrigue there was between Lotta Pettersson and myself
died slowly and painfully and has been extinct for much
longer than the six months we have gone our separate
ways. . .' Now, once more, he'd confirmed the end of
the relationship. And even if it wasn't true it wasn't

her concern, was it? Rune had taken her body. He had never asked her for her heart.

'I'm sorry, you were saying?' Guiltily she banished those disturbing pictures from her mind, to give Rune her full attention.

He was standing against one of the walls of the bedroom, one elbow resting on a long teak shelf which at one time must have contained books, but was now bare, resting his head against the palm of his raised hand in an attitude of relaxation. The pose had thrust his hips sideways as he leant at a slight angle and his free hand was at the level of his pelvis, thumb hooked into the waistband of his jeans, fingers doubled into a loose fist at the top of his hard, powerful thigh.

'I said—have you seen everything you wanted to see?' he repeated softly.

'Yes. Yes, thank you. It's very impressive. Once I have the back-up material, I'm sure I can give you what you want. . .' She was gabbling, her voice breathy and barely under control, because she'd raised her eyes to his face only to find the expression there more disturbing than the casual masculine pose he'd adopted, and which had already reminded her of the night she'd spent in his bed.

It was all there in his eyes as they assessed her confusion—awareness, desire and worst of all a confident masculine knowledge of his own sexual power and her susceptibility to it. She breathed deeply, preparing herself to repulse him if he took a step towards her.

'In that case I suggest we go back to the living-room,' he said easily. 'As you can see from the state of this place, I have someone call in regularly to keep an eye on it. She also sees that there is always something in the drinks cupboard to welcome visitors.'

'Whisky?' she suggested lightly. And was rewarded by an answering grin.

'Among other things.'

She allowed him to lead her back to the living-room, her defences momentarily lapsed so that when he paused on the threshold to slide an arm around her waist and draw her into his embrace she was too shocked to remonstrate.

'Gina, Gina. . .' he murmured, his mouth buried in the thick darkness of her hair, his hands travelling with deep caressing movements up and down her body. 'I vowed to myself not to do this yet, but there's something about you that melts my sternest resolutions.'

Through the thin cotton of her top she could feel their animal warmth, melting her flesh, thawing her own hard-made resolution not to succumb to his practised seduction. She was drawn to him like a magnet to the north. Both of them knew it.

So when he moved slightly to seek her soft lips with his own, blending predatory male purpose with the tenderness of a child seeking succour, she was lost, allowing him to possess her mouth, welcoming him with parted lips, mindlessly enjoying the sensation of his hands as they bound her to him, but not so hard that she couldn't feel their trembling. Instinctively she held his shoulders, allowing her hands freedom to roam across his wide back, trace the strong neck, reach into the thick blond hair. Now she was lost, every cell, every fibre of her body alive with the memory of his possession, aching to re-experience what only a few hours, a few minutes ago she'd sworn to deny them both.

It was Rune who broke the close embrace, lifting his head away, his hands still tender on her shoulders as he scanned her face, his own features harshly set.

'Gina—I think the time has come for me to set the record straight about Lotta and myself. In fact it's one of the reasons I brought you here.' Blue eyes locked with her questioning grey ones, as beside his hard, beautiful masculine mouth two muscles twitched, showing strain. 'For a year and a half we lived here together.' He began to pace the room, hands thrust into pockets, shoulders hunched.

'Rune, you don't have to explain——' she began impulsively.

'Of course I do!' He turned on her fiercely. 'Why do you think I insisted on your staying on here in Denmark when you were hell-bent on leaving? Why do you think I brought you down to his place if it wasn't so that I could stake a claim on your patience—make you listen to what I have to confess because there was no way you could run away from me—flag down a taxi, catch a bus and head for the airport?'

'The air-conditioning unit——' she began hesitantly.

'Damn the air-conditioning unit!' Forcefully he dismissed the genuineness of that as a relevant reason. 'As you said, you could have worked from the literature and specifications I had in the apartment.' He glowered at her, raking a lean, hard hand through his hair. 'Yes, I told you a lie about that. The truth is that I'm finding it damnably hard to confess to you what happened between Lotta and myself, and it's vital that you know.'

'You still love her,' she whispered, voicing her greatest fear. It was a statement, not a question, but he denied it grimly.

'No. What's more, I never did.' He shrugged. 'You've seen her. Physically she's the epitome, almost a caricature of the male fantasy dream girl, and I was stupid enough to endow her with all the other attributes I thought the perfect woman should have.'

Gina smiled gently to hide her own aching despair. 'Which are?'

'Compassion, honesty, integrity and tolerant affection as well as passion.' He glowered down at her, defying her to mock him.

'Oh, Rune. . .' She was nearer to tears than laughter.

'I know.' For a moment she thought she glimpsed a hint of self-mockery soften the hardness of his eyes, then it was gone. 'I was getting on for thirty years of age, with the retarded emotions of an adolescent, and the only excuse I have is that I'd spent most of my youth pursuing excellence rather than women.' He thrust his hands deep into his pockets, hunching his shoulders as he continued, 'I met her at the party I threw to celebrate taking over control of the company. I was elated with the thrill of success. Not only had I gained the technical degree I'd been chasing, but I'd finally achieved a position in a business when I could use that expertise to its full potential. The only sadness was that my parents, who had supported me so fully in the earlier days, weren't there to enjoy my success.'

He paused as if inviting comment but then, when Gina remained silent, her expressive face betraying her thoughts without need of speech, resumed in a softer tone. 'She was a friend of a friend—I hadn't even known she was coming, but one look and I was arrogant enough to decide I was going to make her mine. Looking back, I can see how infantile my behaviour was—but then I was flushed with success, convinced that nothing and no one could thwart me.'

'Rune, please, you don't have to tell me this,' she pleaded, shocked by the emptiness in his eyes as they rested on her.

'You mean you don't want to hear it.' He gazed down at her troubled face. 'But I have to try to make you understand, Gina. It's important to me that you hear my side of the story—though God knows it does me little enough credit! The truth is I pursued Lotta relentlessly, so lost in the thrill of the chase that I didn't realise until too late that we were entirely incompatible. None of it was Lotta's fault at the beginning. She enjoyed being swept off her feet and wooed with such single-minded purpose, her every whim given in to, being inundated with presents.

'When I bought this house and insisted she move in with me she took the path of least resistance and agreed, although even then if I'd had the wits to see them all the signs were there that although she relished my role as provider she cared very little for me as a person.' He laughed, a harsh, bitter sound. 'And who could blame her? I was treating her like some harem favourite and she was repaying me in kind, except that any harem inmate who behaved with Lotta's indiscretion would long since have been tied in a sack and dropped in the Bosporus!' There was a moment's silence as he prowled round the room, his misery betrayed by every contained movement of his lean male body, before he added wryly, 'At the time I was the only man in Copenhagen who didn't know it.' He paused to look around him. 'This was to be my dream home. Instead it turned into a nightmare. Of course, I should put it on the market, but dreams die hard. . .'

Compassion swept through Gina as she responded to the agony of his humiliation, but still she reamined silent, sensing his need to continue his confession without interruption.

'It was several months before the truth finally dawned on me that although I was being entirely faithful to her she had no inhibitions about sleeping with other men for kicks.' Rune's eyes swept across her open face and she saw his jaw tighten momentarily as he clearly read her distress.

'I'm sorry. . .' How inadequate her whispered condolence seemed.

'It was nothing more than I deserved!' Harshly he rejected her sympathy. 'I was forced to face the fact that I was living with a woman I actually disliked and I had no one to blame but myself. I'd coveted Lotta because she was coveted by other men and I had to be the winner. I spent so much effort and expense to outbid my rivals, I never stopped for one moment to consider if I really wanted the prize. Too late I found out that I didn't.'

'But Lotta loved you in her own way?' Oddly, despite her own feelings towards Rune, she could still feel sympathy for the other girl. Female sisterhood, she thought wryly.

'Lotta loved the material things I showered on her,' he retorted drily. 'And of course she was flattered by my undivided attention. Undivided that is except for the demands of my working life. For over a year, because I felt guilty about the way I had trapped her, I tried to make the relationship work, but it was impossible. She really believed I would put up with anything she threw at me just so I could possess her. In previous relationships it had always been Lotta who had moved on to better things; she'd never been rejected before and she felt angry and humiliated, particularly as she saw her standard of living about to fall.' He shrugged. 'In the end she had to realise she couldn't manipulate me—that I didn't love her and never had in the true sense of the word.

'It was then that she showed just how avaricious she was—demanding a half-share of everything I had before she would move out. Because I recognised my own culpability in what had happened I didn't even argue the point.' A wry smile twisted his mouth as he looked around the room. 'I expect you've noticed how empty the house seems. . .'

Gina nodded, remembering the empty bookshelves,

the lack of individual touches which gave character to a house, the paucity of furniture, the lack of movable electronic equipment: no television or video, no state-of-the-art audio system.

'You paid her off,' she said bluntly.

'In the same way as I had bought her,' he agreed bitterly. 'Apart from a few pieces of glass and steel which had been gifts from my family and had sentimental value, I let her run riot among my other acquisitions. I felt it was the least I could do.'

'But not the Knudsen,' Gina reminded him gently.

'Not the Knudsen,' he agreed grimly. 'That was mine. Bought for my own pleasure. Lotta had always hated it, but now she decided she wanted that too.'

'But why, when you'd been so generous. . .?' Bewildered, Gina shook her head.

'Because of its potential value in the future, probably, or even more likely because she wanted to deprive me of something I valued as revenge for what she saw as my dumping her—who knows?'

'But she had no legal claim to it. . .'

'None.' He had stopped prowling to lift a dining chair from its place beside a circular dining table, swinging it round to sit astride it, resting his arms along its back and meeting Gina's quizzical gaze with a rueful smile.

'That wouldn't stop Lotta. When she finally left six months ago I closed this house up and rented the Copenhagen apartment. A few days later I had a visit from her. She put on a great act, pretending to be heartbroken and begging for a chance to restart our relationship, but shortly after she'd gained access to the apartment there was a phone call.

'Fortunately while I was answering it I caught sight of her trying to take the painting down.' He paused, his blue eyes glinting with the first sign of malice he had shown. 'Believe me, she was out of the place before she had time to dry her crocodile tears! Later I discovered she'd arranged for one of her friends to phone and distract me so that she could make off with her booty! She obviously assumed that I wouldn't go to the trouble of prosecuting her once it was in her possession.'

'No wonder you were so suspicious when I arrived unannounced.' Gina put her thoughts into words and was rewarded by a rueful downwards tug of his beautifully chiselled mouth.

'I treated you abominably,' he agreed honestly. 'My only excuse is that I was pretty exhausted after my stay in the Middle East, and not totally reorientated after being awakened after such a short sleep. I really did think Lotta had chosen the day of my return to re-enter the fray!'

He swung one leg over the chair dismounting to replace it, while Gina watched with an aching feeling of sadness the supple play of his muscles, the lithe perfection of his strong body. Perhaps he wasn't without blame, but hadn't she made the same kind of mistake when she had endowed Marcus with the qualities she'd wanted him to possess?

'Ah, *min søde* Gina. . .' He came to her, taking her hands and drawing her to her feet, just standing there looking down at her as she found herself quite incapable of resisting. 'I'd promised I would never fall for the obvious attractions of another beautiful woman, but from the moment I held you in my arms my instinct told me that you were as different from Lotta as wine is from vinegar.'

Oh, dear God, this was more than she could bear! Her mouth dry with anguish, Gina shook her hands free. He was too close, too overpoweringly desirable, and there was no mistaking his physical need for her at that moment. It was etched on every feature of his beloved face, from the dark-pupilled eyes and the slight flush on his high cheekbones to the softness of his mouth.

'No, Rune.' They were the hardest words she'd ever had to say. 'Don't you see you're just repeating history? You've just said that you took one look at Lotta and wanted her without knowing a thing about her, and now you're telling me exactly the same thing. The only good thing about mistakes is that you're supposed to learn from them—not go on making them!'

She pushed him away, closing her eyes to shut out the present image of his face.

'This isn't a mistake.' His whole body seemed to simmer with the power of his protest. 'With Lotta it was a cold-blooded decision to win a woman who would be a beautiful and desirable accessory to my life. In retrospect I admit it was an arrogant, unforgivable thing to do and I've paid the price for it, emotionally and financially. And I'm not unaware of the pain I caused Lotta either. Believe me, I would be truly delighted if she found a new and permanent partner, even though it is difficult to even regard her as a friend after her display of greed, and the wrong impression she deliberately gave you at Ib's Club from sheer vindictiveness. How much longer would you have me pay for my sins, hmm?'

'I'm not judging you.' It was little more than a whisper as Gina flinched from the anguish on his drawn face, every instinct telling her he was speaking the truth, and that Lotta's cruel fabrication had been just that—a compilation of lies in order to destroy what she could no longer possess. 'But I'm not the woman you need to fill the gap Lotta left in your life!'

'Why not?' he asked abrasively. 'You're loyal and unselfish and have a capacity for loving. . .' He raised his hands palms upward in a gesture of despair as his voice thickened with emotion. 'Leave the hotel, move into my apartment. . . Give me a chance to prove I can make you happy!'

How could she accept? He was offering her a few days of physical pleasure which would only leave her thirsty for more. If she wouldn't be able to drink deep it would be better not to take another sip of the heady elixir he offered her. Slowly she shook her head.

'It won't work!' She spoke harshly, taking a step away from him, searching her mind for justification of her rejection. 'What happened last night was a mistake. You said yourself that you regretted it!'

'Yes'. Rune closed the distance between them. 'Because it should never have happened the way it did, but if I was angry it was with myself, not you, because you needed to be courted, to be given time, and I gave you none. My only thought at the time was to wipe out the memory of the ordeal you'd been made to suffer by the man you thought you loved!'

'Well, you certainly did that.' She managed a light laugh but had to blink her eyes to prevent the gathering tears from falling. 'And, believe me, I'm grateful. But that's no reason for repeating the exercise! Now, did you say something about lunch?'

For one poignant second he stood still, his eyes intent on her face, then he was turning away, moving towards the kitchen, saying expressionlessly, 'Of course, if that's the way you want it, Gina.'

CHAPTER TWELVE

IT WAS late evening as the Mercedes entered the immediate environs of Copenhagen, the sinking sun patterning the cirrus-mottled sky with copper rays.

Rune drove well, with the confidence of a man who knew he had nothing to prove about the potential of either himself or his car, Gina conceded as she tried to relax, the soft background music taking the edge off her immediate anxieties about Suzie's whereabouts and safety.

Forcing her mind away from what Rune had told her about the time he'd spent with Lotta and how the relationship had evaporated with only the bitter dregs left in evidence, she allowed it to dwell on how they'd spent the rest of the day.

After lunch in a sheltered spot in the garden she'd vetoed the idea of going sailing, despite Rune's assurance that like many Danes he was a competent sportsman on the water, enjoying water-skiing and sailboarding as well as yachting. She'd never doubted his skill—unless he was a closet body-builder, the well-defined muscle of his body owed their development to regular participation in some kind of sport—only her own ability to keep her untried sea-legs!

Instead she'd accepted his suggestion to show her more of the island of Zealand, and had been enchanted by everything, painfully aware that the spell which had entrapped her emanated from the powerful persona of the man beside her as much as the natural beauty of the surrounding countryside.

Stealing a sideways glance at his profile, she was

unable to quell the *frisson* of excitement which sharpened her perception of him. Suppose she were to change her mind and stay to the end of the week as he had suggested? Would an extra three days really make the final parting that much worse than it was going to be already? She moved restlessly in her seat, torn by an aching indecision.

As if aware of her dilemma, Rune glanced briefly at her before returning his attention to the road ahead.

'Any thoughts about how you want to spend the rest of the evening?' he asked casually. 'Tivoli's open till midnight—but no fireworks tonight; or we could go out to dinner elsewhere. How about a restaurant set in the vaults of a medieval monastry, lit by candles and with a menu that owes its variety to the best raw material found around the world? Or we could go on another tour of the clubs. . .'

'Not the clubs. . .' She shuddered involuntarily. Suppose they should encounter Lotta again? It was a prospect she couldn't face.

'I'm not very hungry. . .' She gazed out of the window aware now of how close they were to the centre of the city and Rune's apartment. 'But I would love to see the ballet performance at the Pantominteatret if there's time.'

'Plenty.' He glanced at the clock on the dashboard as he turned into the courtyard. 'It doesn't start until nine forty-five, so we can have a coffee before we leave.' He paused infinitesimally. 'Perhaps I'll even have time to persuade you not to run away from me after all, *mus*.'

The husky little endearment caught at her heart, as every fibre of her body seemed to respond to his nearness. Had he guessed how badly her emotions were vacillating?

'I've been thinking. . .' They'd reached the door of

the apartment before she broke the silence. 'Since you're having Suzie's trail pursued with such vigour, perhaps it *would* be sensible to stay on until my hotel reservation lapses.'

'That's the best idea you've had all day, *min elskede*!' Rune opened the door propelling her across the threshold, turning her in his arms as he thrust the door closed behind them with his foot. She could have escaped his hold if she'd really wanted to. The compulsion that held her there, head resting against his broad shoulder, she knew was emotional rather than physical. Bewildered by her own inner conflict, she could only stand there feeling totally vulnerable, her limbs barely supporting her as he peered down into her troubled face.

'Gina. . .' His voice was soft, almost a whisper. 'For God's sake tell me the truth. I have to know. Do you want me even half as much as I want you? Last night I was sure you did——'

'No. . .you were right the first time: what happened between us was a dreadful mistake. . .unplanned. I didn't know what I was doing. . .' Desperately she used logic to deny the miracle that had transformed her.

'Ah, Gina—why is it I don't believe you?'

She heard his sigh, then he was raising one hand to the dark wealth of hair at the back of her head, drawing her face away from the warm sanctuary of his chest, ignoring her small whimper of protest as his lips descended on hers.

One taste and she was lost. There wasn't time to edge away or even think as his mouth possessed her and his hands moved on her body, caressing it beneath the soft folds of her cotton top. Instinctively she clung to him, indifferent to everything but the powerful clamouring of her heart, the vibrant response of her senses to the sweet pleasure of his nearness. It was madness, but it was a sweet madness more enthralling than her previous lonely sanity.

As her body confirmed what he'd already guessed she had neither the will nor wit to attempt to deny it any more. She was shaking when his mouth finally drifted away from hers, her heart beating with increased rapidity as he smiled down into her flushed face, gazing intently at her dark-pupilled eyes with their luminous circles of grey iris.

'Admit it, *min skat*,' he chided her softly. 'Is it so difficult to put into words what I can read on your face? Surely you no longer suspect me of using you in some devious plan to make Lotta jealous?'

Gina shook her head. 'No, but after what you told me I have a suspicion you kissed me that night at Ib's Club deliberately in an effort to convince her you'd found someone else to replace her in your heart and in your bed.' She offered him a wry smile.

He expelled his breath in a long exhalation.

'And, if I did, what of it? It was true, wasn't it?'

'Was it?' She raised pain-filled eyes to meet his stern regard. 'When you'd already made the low opinion in which you held both me and my sister crystal-clear?'

'I was angry!' he admitted, thrusting his hands into the pockets of his trousers as he studied her, his eyes traversing her slender form, raking over the tangle of dark hair, her susceptible grey eyes, her full, sensual mouth, before lowering them in slow appraisal of her trim figure then returning them to her querulous expression. 'Damn it, Gina. It wasn't the best news to come home to—finding my renegade nephew had not only broken and entered my apartment but was bent on destroying an important career opportunity by eloping with some feather-brained teenager! I'm afraid I spilled my temper out on you.' He scowled and once more she was forcibly reminded of his Viking heritage, the cold, hard power that had fortified the Norsemen as they had bounded from their makeshift camps intent on conquest. With Rune's jaw hard and his mouth set in a straight line it was easy to imagine just how terrifying their enemies had found the invaders.

'Besides,' he continued, 'when you first burst into my life I was disillusioned, bruised, doubtful of my own judgement where women were concerned. I'd resolved that the next woman I let into my life would be chosen with my mind and my heart—not my eyes and my libido!' Unsmiling, his light blue eyes commanded her attention, mesmerising her where she stood. 'But no, Gina. I swear to you that when I kissed you in Ib's Club it was simply because I couldn't resist the temptation. The first time had been in anger—the second time something very different. At the time I'd no idea Lotta was even there.' He grimaced. 'Believe me, she was the very last person I wanted to see.'

'Last night you accused me of importuning the young man on the canal boat!' She thrust her chin upward in mock anger, delighted to have him on the defensive.

'Impure, unreasonable jealousy,' he admitted heavily. 'I was furious when I got to the hotel that morning to find you'd already left. But even as I made it I knew my accusation was ridiculous. By the end of that first evening I'd discovered that, however much of a rebel your younger sister might be, *you* were made of tougher, truer stool.'

'That's absurd.' Gina tried to laugh as his softly delivered judgement made her heart lurch. Of course he wasn't serious, it was just a way of flirting, but she couldn't let his statement go unchallenged. 'You don't know anything about me.' Except, a small protective inner voice prompted her hurtfully, that I'm no long-term threat to your person or your property because in a few days' time at the very most I shall be out of your land and out of your life.

His laugh was soft as he clasped her hand to draw her further into the room. 'I know everything I need to know about you, *mus*,' he told her gently. 'Inside that defensive shield you've built around you, you have a warm and generous spirit and a great capacity for loving. . . What more could any man ask of a woman? Especially a Dane whose idea of total happiness is to be *hyggelig*?'

'Oogerly?' Her stab at phonetic pronunciation brought laughter to his eyes.

'Warm, cosy, contented. . .it's a very Danish word, difficult to translate.' When he pulled her, unresisting, into his embrace, her head settled against his collarbone as one hand splayed tenderly across her back. 'Don't run away from me, Gina. Let's enjoy the time we have left together. There's so much I want to share with you, *min kaere*: so much I want to show you, and not only in bed. . .'

Curiously husky, his voice beguiled her ears as powerfully as his hands were seducing her body, caressing her naked skin beneath her simple top, tantalising the sensitised surface, warm and demanding, seeking the clasp of her flesh-coloured bra, dismantling it with a sure touch that might have come from practice but could equally well have been attributed to simple deduction, except that nothing was simple about this man who had already knowingly conquered her body . . .and, unknowingly, her heart as well.

She was lost—and he knew it, sighing with a deep satisfaction as she stirred against him, enabling him to cup her warm, pulsating breasts in his palms.

'*Min skat, min elskede*. . .ah, Gina, *jeg elsker dig*. . .' He was breathing the words against her skin, his voice muffled by the folds of cotton he had pushed aside to enable his mouth to cherish the tender apices of her pale breasts.

Straining away from him, gasping with tortured gratification, she found that it seemed the most natural thing in the world to her when she was swept up in his arms and carried through into the bedroom, to be laid gently down on the soft duvet. Covering her with his own body, he abolished all remnants of coherent thought as he parted her lips with his own, possessing her mouth with a mixture of passion and tenderness. Loving her with his hands and his mouth, disrobing her with an erotic skill that brought her flesh to fire, he discarded his own clothes with an economy of movement, revealing his body to her in all the beauty of its prime, before embarking on a journey of initiation which had her sobbing his name.

Instinctively she knew how to pleasure him in return, exalted when he moaned at the delicacy of her touch and begged for her to increase the pressure of her caresses, until they reached the point of no return together, their bodies joining in a union so satisfying, so complete that in that moment of culmination Gina no longer felt a separate entity. In that endless moment she was truly a part of Rune, sharing his strength of mind and body, his former pain and his present pleasure.

Afterwards, she lay naked, warm and quiescent in the curve of his arm, listening to his laboured breathing, feeling the fast, steady beat of his heart as it thundered against her cheek, knowing that it could never have been so good, so satisfying for both of them if she hadn't loved him.

Raising herself on one arm, she stared down at his face, absorbing every detail of it, admiring the hard bones, the strong yet soft lines of his mouth, the twin fans of eyelashes resting against his cheekbones as, eyes closed, he waited, as all men must, for his strength to return after such an explosion of passionate need.

What did it matter if there would be no long-term future for them together—that in a few days' time they would be separated by the cold grey expanse of the North Sea? He had wooed her with hunger tempered with tenderness, lifting her to heights of fulfilment she could never have even imagined before she had met him, and she'd been a willing, eager vessel, wreaking her woman's power over him, submitting joyfully to his possession until in the final moment of consummation she had robbed him of his strength, leaving him as helpless as Samson shorn of his crowning glory.

Her hand strayed to touch his short thick hair, a small yelp of surprise escaping her as her wrist was grasped by strong fingers and she found herself looking down into alert blue eyes.

'I thought you were asleep!' she accused breathlessly.

'No, just trying to decide whether I should take you riding in a horse-drawn carriage through Dyrhaven tomorrow, or whether I should spend the whole day making love to you.'

Her heart flipped alarmingly. Dared she suggest a compromise? Instead she stretched lazily, conscious of his eyes lingering admiringly on her pale curves.

'I may decide to fly back to England tomorrow after all,' she lied teasingly. 'I have a very important campaign to get off the ground.'

'I think perhaps I can persuade you to delay that, *min elskede*,' he returned lazily. 'You see, I have yet an alternative proposition to put to you.'

'Now?' She raised querulous eyebrows, enjoying the faster recuperative power of her sex. 'It must be true after all, what they say about Viking lovers!'

'What do they say, Gina?'

He pulled her down hard on top of him, clamping

her against his relaxed body, pinioning her in place with the formidable strength of his golden-skinned legs, winding one hand through her dishevelled hair to control her even further. She struggled for the sheer fun of it, disappointed as her futile gasps and gyrations were interrupted by the shrilling of the doorbell.

Rune muttered what could only have been a string of invective in his own language as he released his hold on her.

'I suppose I'd better see who it is,' he said savagely as she rolled away from him, allowing him to ease himself off the bed to gather his trousers from the floor. 'It might be important.'

Feasting her eyes on him as he quickly enclosed his nether limbs, Gina was forcibly reminded of their first meeting. How could she have possibly imagined how dramatically her feelings towards him would have changed in so short a time?

She had imagined the unwelcome caller would be quickly repulsed, but after ten minutes, when she could still hear the sound of voices in the outer room, she reluctantly left the bed to enter the shower, and was fully clothed and brushing her hair in front of the bedroom mirror by the time the door opened to re-admit Rune.

'At last!' she scolded affectionately. 'Who was it—someone selling double-glazing or insurance?' Then she caught sight of his reflection, and turned to face him, all the colour draining from her face at the harsh expression which sharpened the well-cut bones of his face. 'Rune, what is it? What's happened? Oh, dear God—don't say it's anything to do with Svend and Suzie!' She moved towards him, clutching at his arms in her anxiety.

'Relax, sweetheart.' He grasped her shoulders tenderly. 'It's good news. Suzie is back home safe and sound in England.'

'How. . .who. . .?' Words failed her.

'It was Svend at the door,' Rune explained evenly. 'It appears there'd been a big row and a parting of the ways before my agent tracked them down, but my premise was right: they'd been staying with one of Svend's college friends at his parents' apartment on the outskirts of the city. He tells me he was sharing a room with his friend while Suzie had a bed in his friend's sister's room. Apparently all went well for a few days, then Svend's conscience got the better of him. He got to thinking how disappointed his parents would be if he didn't go back to Fyn in time to meet his father's cousin.'

'And Suzie objected?' Gina asked sadly. It would be typical of her young sister not to be able to see anyone else's point of view. Pretty, dramatic Suzie, who could twist the younger members of the male sex round her beautifully manicured fingers, would have made it a point of honour to test her feminine power over Svend. It seemed on this occasion she had met her match.

Rune nodded. 'Svend wasn't very forthcoming, but the outcome was that Suzie packed her bags and left Copenhagen in high dudgeon yesterday morning. He was putting a bold face on it but I suspect he's taking the parting quite badly—at least he had the grace to phone your sister's home last night to confirm that she'd arrived safely.'

'Oh, heavens—Margaret probably rang my hotel last night to let me know. Whatever must she be thinking?'

'That you spent the night on the tiles?' Rune suggested with the glimmer of a smile momentarily transforming his stern face. 'You're hardly a teenager who has to explain herself to her mother.'

'No, of course I don't.,' she snapped. 'It's simply a

matter of courtesy. I shall have to phone her straight away.'

'Be my guest.' Pulling the door open further, Rune waved her towards the outer room and the telephone. 'I'll find the country code for you.'

Waiting impatiently while he found an International Dialling Code leaflet, Gina tapped her fingers in a nervous tattoo against the wall, her previous euphoria shattered by the welcome but unexpected news.

'The first Svend knew that there was a search on for Suzie and himself was when my agent arrived at the house earlier this evening,' Rune told her calmly as he sorted through a small pile of leaflets. 'Svend was watching television and nursing his broken heart, trying to work out how he could go back home without losing face, when he was forced to realise the amount of trouble and disruption he and his erstwhile girlfriend had caused on all fronts!'

'Well, at least he did the right thing in coming here,' Gina allowed. 'Especially when he must have guessed the kind of reception he'd get.'

'He can count his good luck that he didn't come a few minutes earlier,' Rune said crisply. 'In the circumstances, although I could have wished he'd delayed his visit another hour or so, the edge of my temper had become somewhat dulled by recent events. Although I left him in no doubts about my opinion of his behaviour over the past few weeks, I wasn't quite as brutal with him as I might have been. Besides,' he added with a cruel smile twisting his mobile mouth, 'by the looks of him he'd already had his share of suffering. It seems that the seductive Suzie gave him a hard time one way and another.'

'No more than he deserved, probably,' Gina remarked tartly. 'I would have liked to meet him.'

'And I'm sure he would have reciprocated the

pleasure, *mus*, especially if you'd still been in the same state of undress as you were when I left you. Here— here's the code for England. Dial this first, then your area code minus the first zero, followed by your home number.' He handed her the leaflet, an odd appraising smile playing about his mouth.

'Thanks.' Gina followed his instructions, as he strolled away towards the kitchen, delighted when she got the ringing tone at her first attempt. The last thing she wanted now was to discuss her own behaviour over the past hour—or the past days come to that!

'Margaret?' The carefully enunciated tones of her mother's telephone voice were unmistakable.

'Gina! Thank heavens. I wasn't sure if that girl at the reception desk understood my message when I asked you to phone me. Suzie's back home! Quite unharmed by her experience but suffering from a fit of the sulks. I'm sorry you've had a wasted journey. Still, it made a nice little break for you.'

'Yes, it did,' Gina agreed as her mother paused for breath. Although 'nice' was hardly the word for the brief joy she had found in the fairy-tale city.

'I imagine Suzie will soon bounce back,' Margaret continued, clearly uninterested in her elder daughter's experiences. 'As a matter of fact your father's been in touch with us.' Her voice was edged with excitement. 'Some mad plan he's into to build a golf course in Cornwall. He actually suggested he and I go down there together to look it over. When we get back you'll have to come over. I'm sure he'd love to see you again after all these years.'

Biting back a retort to the effect that it was doubtful if Campion Price would even recognise her, Gina said equably, 'I'll try to fit a visit in.'

'Good—oh, here's Suzie now demanding to speak to you.'

'Gina? Oh, Gina, when are you coming home?' Hysteria and misery mingled in Suzie's light voice. 'I don't know what to do. I'm so miserable I cried all the way home. We were going to be married—Svend and me—at least I thought we were. I thought he loved me! He said all these marvellous things to me, told me how beautiful I was and how there would never be another girl in the world for him. . .' Her voice broke, the flow of words interrupted by painful sobs.

'Suzie, darling. . .' Gina clutched the receiver more tightly. 'Suzie, what is it—are you pregnant?'

'No!' The denial was more bitter than relieved. 'I wish I was, then he'd have had to marry me. He was such great fun when we met, then suddenly it all changed. He wouldn't even make love to me, not properly, that is. He said it wouldn't be fair on me because he had to finish his exams first before he could get seriously involved with me!'

'That sounds a responsible attitude,' Gina suggested gently, deciding not to comment unfavourably on her sister's naïve comment about marriage being the inevitable consequence of pregnancy. Now was not the time to preach.

'He just didn't love me enough,' Suzie wailed. 'So when he told me he had to go back home to Fyn to meet someone, but that I could go with him if I wanted, I gave him an ultimatum.' Her breath sawed as she tried to control her tears, while Gina waited despairingly, knowing what the outcome had been. 'I told him if he wouldn't stay in Copenhagen with me than I was catching the first plane home!'

'Oh Suzie. . .' Gina bit her lip as her sister's anguished sobs echoed over the line. If only she could be with her, give her a hug, the affection and understanding she needed, at the same time trying to make her see that issuing ultimatums inevitably led to war—whether it was between countries or lovers!

'When will you be home, Gina?' Again the agonised question. 'Dad's coming over here and he and Mum are going down to Cornwall. Honestly, you'd think it was Antony coming back for Cleopatra the way she's carrying on!' Another half-subdued sob. 'She doesn't even care that I'm so depressed—I wish I were dead!'

The dream was fading, images of the Royal Deer Park and horse-drawn carriages dissolving, the anticipation of three more nights spent in Rune's arms melting away as Suzie's muted sobs carried across the distance between them. How could she indulge herself when Suzie was so distressed? What she and Rune had shared had been wonderful, exhilarating. He would always have a special place in her heart for as long as she lived; but Rune didn't need her and Suzie did. Even then the decision wasn't easy. She'd never realised she possessed such a deep core of selfishness. Her eyes closed for a brief second as she drew all her inner strength together to steady her voice.

'Listen, Suzie. We were all very worried about you and I'm delighted you're home again. Margaret was nearly out of her mind when she asked me to come out here to look for you, but that's all in the past now. Since there's no reason for me to stay in Denmark any longer, I'll try to get a flight home tomorrow. Then you must come over and stay with me and tell me everything that's happened. With a bit of luck we'll be able to make a holiday of it for you, get in a couple of London shows as well.'

'You're not angry with me, then?' There was a note of hope in Suzie's voice.

'No,' Gina confirmed wearily. 'No, Suzie, I'm not angry. With a bit of luck I'll see you tomorrow.'

She replaced the receiver, standing unmoving,

staring across the room towards the Knudsen with hungry eyes, knowing it was the last time she would ever see it.

'Coffee, Gina?'

Rune was standing by the table, a mug in each hand, his naked torso gleaming in the light streaming from the kitchen, his face cold and reserved. Gone was the strong, fiery Viking lover. In his place the cool, detached Dane who had taken nothing she hadn't been prepared to give—and given nothing she hadn't been prepared to take.

'Thank you.' It was little more than a whisper as she walked towards him. 'Rune, I've been talking to Suzie. . .'

'Yes, I caught the end of your conversation,' he responded expressionlessly. 'I'll phone the airport now for you and see what's available while you drink your coffee. Do you have a preference between Gatwick and Heathrow?'

'No. Whichever gets in first.' She cleared her throat, damning it for its sudden huskiness. Why should she have hoped even for one split second that Rune would attempt to persuade her to change her mind—not that he would have succeeded?

His finger was fast on the dial pad, his blue gaze unwavering as he lifted the phone to his ear, as he cast her an oblique glance. 'When the travel arrangements are settled I'll drive you straight back to your hotel. I imagine you'll want to pack and have an early night.'

CHAPTER THIRTEEN

'A HEADACHE?' Grantham and Marsh's top account director stared at Gina with disbelief. 'For pity's sake, Gina, can't you take an aspirin or something? What the hell is this Christensen guy going to think if you don't turn up at his party?'

'That I've got a headache, presumably, since that's what you're going to tell him, Adrian,' Gina said wearily. 'Look, you can see I've made the effort.' She gestured down at the pale lilac, close-fitting, long-sleeved light wool jersey dress she was wearing. 'But it's no good, I just don't feel up to it. It's just a tension headache. What I need is a couple of hours' peace and quiet and I'll be fine for the presentation tomorrow—besides,' she added persuasively, 'it's not as if the party was being thrown for us. My not being there is hardly likely to lose us the account if Ru——' She stopped herself just in time. 'If Herre Christensen likes what we've done when he sees the full campaign tomorrow.'

'Yeah, I guess she's right.' Nigel Barrowfield, the art director and third member of the agency's delegation to Denmark, nodded sagely. 'It's just coincidence that we're ready to make our presentation on the second anniversary of Christensen's buying out the original company. From what I heard, all the employees of the company will be there, some four hundred or so, so our little Gina, beautiful though she is, will hardly be missed.' He leered at her, then almost immediately his face took on an air of concern. 'Sure you'll be OK if we leave you, sweetheart?' He glanced around the large, pleasant room in the first-class hotel that had been booked for her. 'Anything you need or want, just ring the bell. Don't forget you're Seb's blue-eyed grey-eyed girl of the hour, so the sky's the limit on expenses!'

'Only if we pull the deal off.' She smiled wanly. 'Mustn't count our chickens, Nige.'

'Rubbish!' It was Adrian who interposed. 'What with your clever copy, Nige's brilliant artwork and my own masterminding over the past couple of months, we're home and dry—and air-conditioned!' He laughed at his own joke. 'We'll be seeing ya, kid!'

As the door of her room closed behind them, Gina released her breath in a deep sigh of relief. She really had made an effort to accept Rune's invitation for the three of them to attend the firm's party on the eve of their campaign presentation, but at the last moment her nerve had failed her. Tomorrow would be a business presentation, no different from the many she had already attended for other campaigns. She was word-perfect in the part she had to play; knew she could perform without betraying her nervousness. But tonight would have been different.

All through the short plane journey she'd been imagining what it would be like to meet Rune again socially. How would he greet her—as a friend or a near stranger? Seven weeks and five days since that cataclysmic day when Svend had interrupted their lovemaking, and she had heard nothing from him. Not that she'd expected to. She shivered, her right hand moving restlessly towards the gold chain with its rectangular pendant which lay on the exposed skin of her neck above the scooped-out neckline of her dress: Rune's parting gift given to her that dull morning when, after having insisted on collecting her from her hotel, he had driven her to the airport at Kastrup.

He had waited with her in the elegant departure

lounge with its striking shopping centre and attractive bars and cafés, until her flight was called. As far as she could remember they'd spent the time discussing potential ideas for his proposed advertising campaign. Then at the last moment he'd pressed the small jeweller's box into her hand. 'It's a *guldgubber*,' he'd explained shortly. 'A memento of your stay in Copenhagen. *Farvel*, Gina.' Then, before she'd had time to express her thanks, he'd touched her cheek briefly with his warm, dry lips and stridden away, leaving her feeling lonely and bereft, the small box clasped in her hand. She'd waited the few moments it took for his lean, athletic figure to be swallowed up in the crowd, feasting her eyes on his receding back, fighting back the threatening tears.

On the plane she'd examined the pendant cut from sheet gold on which two primitive figures were carved in relief. It was obviously expensive, but then Rune was used to paying his lovers off, wasn't he? Nevertheless she'd put it round her neck and there it had stayed ever since while she'd tried with scant success to forget the brief period of ecstasy she'd shared with the man whose gift it had been.

How could she possibly have walked into the reception room at the hotel where Rune was holding his anniversary party and looked him in the face without betraying the fact that despite the passage of time and distance she still loved him? Tomorrow would be different, would have to be different. Tomorrow she would take on the persona of Gina Price, hard, successful career-girl, polished and rehearsed, bright, shiny and heart-whole!

Tonight—ah, tonight. Tonight she had other plans. Her plea of a headache had not been entirely false. But she had a better way of relaxing the tightness that started at the back of her neck and spread across the crown of her head than attempting sleep.

She allowed herself ten minutes for Nigel and Adrian to get clear of the hotel before slipping her arms into a grey mohair jacket, collecting her shoulder-bag and slipping quietly out of the hotel.

The streets of the city welcomed her as an old friend as she made her way unerringly towards the brilliantly lit entrance of Tivoli. The late summer air was surprisingly mild as she passed through the turnstiles into the 'enchanted garden'. Looking around her, she could perceive little difference in the appearance of the gardens since her last visit. The flowers still bloomed as brightly in early September as they had in July, the crowds still sat in the open-air cafés. Perhaps some wore jackets this time and perhaps some restaurants pampered their customers with radiant ceiling heating slanting down on their open galleries, but the Tivoli lights still swung as gently in the trees, the musicians played as sweetly, and the Pantominteatret still stood in all its glory, its magnificent 'curtain' of a peacock with fan-shaped tail unfurled waiting dramatically against a sky of indigo velvet for the second performance of the evening. If she did sense an added aura of poignancy it was probably because in less than two weeks Tivoli would close its turnstiles and remain dormant until its spring awakening at the end of the following April.

Too early for the ballet, Gina wandered around giving herself up to the magic of the gardens, walking round the lake where large metal dragon-flies appeared to hover as the flickering lights in their wings simulated movement.

When the famous peacock screen folded its tail and disappeared into the floor of the stage and the small orchestra began to play she was ready and waiting, standing on the slight rise looking directly at a stage which appeared suspended in the air against the night sky.

No matter that she had no idea of the story behind the dance, she watched entranced for the half-hour as the orchestra played, fauns cavorted, lovers kissed and villains fought. It was over much too soon, the music climaxing as some deity descended from the heavens and a pyramid of angels formed with waving chiffon drapes, the stage throbbed with soft lights and the lovers embraced.

She stood there until the rapturous applause died down and the peacock screen rose from the floor, hiding all behind it, then, her eyes clouded by emotional tears conjured up by the sheer beauty of what she had just witnessed, she turned blindly, colliding with a hard male body.

'*Undskyld!*' Glad that her limited knowledge of Danish included an apology, she blinked away her tears, raising her eyes to the stranger's face and freezing as completely as Lot's wife as she found herself looking into the ice-blue eyes of the man she loved. 'Rune?' His name choked in her throat.

'Why the tears, Gina?' he asked gently. 'It's supposed to be a happy ending.'

'Why—why aren't you at the party?' she asked tremulously, her thought processes shattered by shock, as she registered the formal pale grey suit he was wearing, the immaculate white shirt and grey and maroon tie.

'Why aren't you?' he responded gently.

'I had a headache. . .' Silently her eyes pleaded for him to believe her.

'And I had a heartache, *mus*.' He regarded her steadily. 'For nearly two months I've been counting the days until I would see you again. Can you have any idea how I felt when your colleagues walked in alone?'

She shook her head. She'd imagined her absence wouldn't have been remarked upon. Nigel and Adrian were the high-powered executives; her non-appearance at a social gathering was hardly noteworthy. 'I did ask them to explain and apologise for me,' she offered, anxious not to prejudice all the hard work the agency had put in.

'Oh, they did.' He was contemplating her worried expression with a faint smile curling his mouth. 'And I spent an hour greeting my guests, making a speech and ensuring the entertainment was fully organised for the evening, while I was trying to make up my mind whether your refusal to put in an appearance was because you cared for me—or because you hated me.'

'I had. . .' she began desperately.

'An attack of nerves,' he supplemented softly. 'And I was determined to find out why. So as soon as I could get away I went to your hotel, only to be told that you had left shortly after your colleagues.'

'I thought the fresh air——'

Again his deep voice cut across her explanation. 'So I asked myself, where would you go? And I remembered our last day together when I'd promised to bring you to the Peacock theatre and robbed you of your heart's desire by forcing you into my bed instead. So I asked myself where else would you be but at Tivoli watching the ballet?'

'You didn't force me. I went willingly.' She lifted her dark head high, determined to meet him on equal terms. 'Surely you didn't think I bore you any personal grudge about what happened?'

'I certainly hoped not.' He reached out a hand to touch the charm at her throat. 'I see you still wear the *guldgubber*.'

'It's a very unusual piece of jewellery. Many people have commented on it. I'm sorry you didn't give me enough time to thank you for it.'

'There was no need for thanks, Gina.' The blue eyes smiled tantalisingly. 'That you wear it is sufficient for my purpose. Did you know it's a replica of one of the charms said to be over a thousand years old and dug up on the island of Bornholm?'

'No, I didn't.' She touched the pendant with curious fingers, hoping she could keep the conversation impersonal. Obviously Rune must have thought she harboured some grudge against him and had been anxious to prevent a potential display of hostility in front of his colleagues the next day. A wave of disappointment surged through her. How could he even contemplate she might behave badly?

'Perhaps we should take a little walk,' he suggested mildly. 'The lake is lovely at night. *Kom*!'

She flinched as his arm slid round her waist, but he showed no sign that he had sensed her withdrawal, asking instead, 'And how is your sister?'

'Oh, Suzie's fine.' Glad that the conversation had moved to a wide field, she gave a sigh of relief. 'My father's deeply involved in setting up a golf course in Cornwall and he's taken Margaret and Suzie down there with him. From what I hear they're both having the time of their lives! My father has been buying Margaret a designer wardrobe and escorting her to all the best restaurants and clubs and Suzie has taken up surf-boarding. She's had such a good time and made so many new friends that she's quite resigned to going back to school in a few days' time.'

Her face glowed with pleasure for her family's happiness. Campion Price really did seem to be a reformed character and Margaret was positively glowing, all the care she had taken over her appearance in the bad years paying handsome dividends, particularly now her lovely eyes were bright with a long-hidden joy.

'And Svend?' she asked, trying to fight down the growing awareness of Rune's hard body so close to her own, the feel of his hand against her waist, the slight rubbing of their thighs as he measured his pace to match her own.

'In the States,' he replied succinctly. 'Naturally, Hanne and Jens are delighted.' He slid her a sly look. 'And ever since Lotta Pettersson decided to go back to Sweden I can enjoy my Knudsen without worrying about its safekeeping.'

Gina's heart skipped a little beat as he answered the question she was too proud to ask. Why had he come here to find her? Was there more to it than she'd supposed? The hotel rooms for herself and her colleagues had been reserved through Rune's secretary so he would know they intended to stay until Sunday— four nights. It had been meant to give time for negotiation if there were problems about their proposed campaign. It would also give time for Rune to inveigle her into taking up their affair where it had left off. That must never happen! Seven weeks had elapsed, and her self-inflicted wounds were still as raw as the day that she'd left. If Rune hadn't insisted on her presence at the presentation she would still be in England. Oh, dear lord, how she wished she were.

'What is it Gina?' He had sensed her unease, stopping in his stride to swing her round to face him.

'Nothing!' Her reply was too fast, too slick.

'Is it Grantham and Marsh?' He frowned. 'The reports I've been receiving suggest they're well on the road to recovery.'

'They are,' she hastened to assure him. 'Once the rumour spread that we'd been asked to put forward a campaign for a Danish-based company with worldwide interests, we suddenly became very popular.' She met his gaze frankly. 'Whatever your decision tomorrow about the work we've done on your behalf, Grantham and Marsh will survive.'

'You can't imagine how pleased that makes me feel, *mus*.' He raised his right hand to trace the line of her cheekbone, running the back of his thumb across her soft parted lips. 'I wouldn't want to be responsible for their collapse.'

'You've already made up your mind not to give them your account?' The sheer unfairness of it brought a flush of angry colour to her cheeks. 'Even before you've seen the presentation? Oh, Rune—how could you be so, so—unscrupulous? We've put blood, sweat and tears into this campaign and now you're dismissing it out of hand!'

'No.' His smile was enigmatic. 'I have no intention of robbing Grantham and Marsh of their triumph if they deserve it, and from what I hear of their reputation they probably will. All I intend to do is rob them of their chief copywriter.'

'I don't undersatand.' It was barely a whisper as Rune guided her to a seat half hidden by luxuriant foliage. 'You're offering me a job?'

'Yes, sweet Georgina Price. . .' He took both her unresisting hands in his. 'I want you to spend the rest of your life with me, here, in Denmark.'

'But. . .' She stared at him uncomprehendingly. Was this his way of asking her to take over Lotta's place in his life? 'Margaret—Suzie. . .'

'Are quite able to look after themselves! Damn it, Gina. . .' He pulled her roughly to her feet. 'We can't talk here. Let's go back to my apartment.'

Like a zombie she let him lead her from Tivoli, allowed him to fasten the seatbelt of the Mercedes round her, followed him into the apartment, standing motionless while he switched on the soft wall lighting.

'Gina. . .*min søde* Gina. . .' He approached her still figure, drawing her into his arms, nestling her head against his strong shoulder. 'I'm asking you to marry me, be my wife. . .fill all the empty places in my life, as I will do my utmost to fill all those in yours.' His hands moved convulsively up and down her back. 'I love you, Gina. I want to be so many things in your life—your lover, your husband, the father of your children.'

'Rune—I——' She grabbed at his shoulders for support as her head swam. She'd half expected he would want to make love with her again, had felt her own body liquefy with musky desire for him. Had already admitted to herself the extent of her own love for him. But to be his wife. . .

'Marriage?' The question trembled on her tongue. 'But you never got in touch with me after I left. . .' She shook her dark head despairingly. 'I thought— believed it was a passing affair. . .'

'I had to give you time! Gina, listen to me!' He took her firmly by the shoulders. 'Do you remember our last day together—the last time we made love—just before Svend rang the bell? I told you I had a proposition to put to you. Well, that was it. I was going to ask you to marry me.' He shook his head. 'Then all your family worries descended on your lovely shoulders and I decided not to add to that burden. I thought you needed breathing space—besides, I'd already ensured you would return with my advertising campaign—and also I'd taken one extra precaution.' His eyes were full of mischief as she gazed enquiringly at him. 'I put you under the influence of a powerful Viking spell which ensured you would be faithful to me.' He touched the golden necklet which encircled her throat. 'The small engraved figures are those of Frey, the Nordic god of fertility embracing his beloved. The pendant is said to ensure fertility and a happy marriage—not necessarily in that order.'

'Oh!' She moved her own hand towards her neck only to have it seized by Rune's. 'I had no idea. . .' Gazing into the depths of his eyes, she tried to read his soul. 'You—you never once told me you loved me.'

He laughed, a brief explosion of sound in the quiet room. 'More than once, sweet Georgina Price. Unfortunately I forgot to translate it into English, but you may remember—*jeg elsker dig*. . .?'

'*Jeg elsker dig*. . .' Wonderingly she repeated the phrase. Yes, she did remember.

'Again,' he implored, his hands moving to cup her breasts. 'Say it again!'

'Oh, Rune!' She obliged with pleasure. '*Jeg elsker dig, jeg elsker dig*!'

She would have said it a third, even a fourth time, but he sealed her mouth with his own, possessing its sweetness with a plunderer's purpose. Against her yielding flesh she could feel his heart thundering like a man who had run a marathon.

'*Min kaere Gud mus*!' He dispossessed her mouth, trailing his open lips across her cheek to whisper in her ear. 'You can't believe how happy I am to hear you say that. I was so afraid tonight when you didn't show up that I'd made the biggest mistake of my life in letting you go back to England without trying to extract a promise from you.' He hugged her close to him, pressing his hands down her body, his own rampant masculinity hunting blatantly against her yielding female flesh. 'You're truly my heart's desire—honest, loving and giving. . .and so very, very beautiful.' His voice was hoarse with a barely controlled desire. 'I want to spend the rest of my life making you happy.'

'And we'll be *hyggelig*?' Gina suggested teasingly, her heart overflowing with joy as every fibre in her body responded to him.

'And much more. . .' He caught her up in his arms, carrying her through to the bedroom, disrobing her with eager, predatory fingers until she stood naked except for the glint of gold at her throat.

She was trembling, aflame with a happiness so great she thought she could never contain it as Rune discarded his own clothes with such rapidity and lack of care that two shirt buttons fell unheeded on to the carpet.

They came together with pride and passion, each glorying in the belief that Hans Christian Andersen had been right and that their fairy-tale had indeed been written by the fingers of God and come to fruition in the Enchanted Garden that had captured the heart of a city. In the heady fire of consummation Gina knew that the aching loneliness which had dogged her throughout her life was finally ended, her own desire rising to match Rune's as their mutual need drowned them in the remorselessly rising tide of satisfaction.

'Gina?' With gentle fingers he smoothed her damp hair away from her clear forehead. 'You still haven't given me your answer.'

'Answer?' Puzzled, she met his intense gaze through love-dazed eyes. 'What was the question?'

'Will you marry me, *mus*?'

'Oh, *that* question. . .' She lowered her lashes and sighed deeply, prolonging the moment from a sense of fun; and then she saw his face, glimpsed the uncertainty there and knew the time for games was over.

The ecstasy she'd felt the night Rune had ensured the silence of the *lur* blowers in City Hall Square had overpowered and exhilarated her, but now it was eclipsed by the knowledge that he loved her. He'd sought her out in her sanctuary, confirmed her belief with the tender, arousing touch of the perfect lover, and she'd learned enough from him to return his caresses with a woman's intimate knowledge of how to pleasure the body of the man she loved. With a deep, reassuring certainty Gina knew that for both of them the rhapsody of love was only just beginning.

'*Ja*,' she said. '*Ja, min elskede!*'

And after that brief excursion into the mysterious tongue of her beloved she said very little else for a considerable time.

COPENHAGEN

Whether you intend to have a quiet weekend with your loved one or prefer a place with lots to do, Copenhagen is an ideal city to visit! Considered to be the oldest kingdom in the world, Denmark is a country which has something for everyone and Copenhagen is no exception. Walks around the city can be combined with special sightseeing tours, followed by a leisurely meal with some lively entertainment—the possibilities are endless! This is the perfect city for setting your own pace, and however you choose to spend your time your enjoyment is guaranteed.

THE ROMANTIC PAST

The name Copenhagen or Kobenhavn is derived from 'Merchants' Harbour', first mentioned in 1043 as a small fishing and trading port on the Oresund, the stretch of water between Sweden and Denmark. However, in 1417, with the aim of returning trade to Denmark, the capital was moved from Roskilde to Copenhagen, where it has remained ever since.

Denmark is a country full of history and legend. Visitors can view the **Caritas fountain** with its annual tradition, dating from the Golden Wedding of King Christian IX and Queen Louise in 1892, to make imitation golden apples dance on the jets on the monarch's birthday, which is now on April 16.

You can also visit the **Gefion fountain**, which commemorates the legendary founding of the Island of Zealand, on which Copenhagen is built. Legend has it that it was ploughed by the goddess from the mainland of Sweden as a result of a bet with the King!

Lovers of Shakespeare will be keen to visit **Elsinore Castle** (Helsingør), which is only a few miles outside Copenhagen and is where *Hamlet* was set!

One of the most famous sights in Copenhagen is the statue of the Little Mermaid (*Den Lille Havfrue*); she sits on a clump of rocks overlooking the harbour. In Andersen's fairy-tale, the mermaid sacrificed her voice in exchange for human legs so that she could win the love of a prince, but then, being mute, was helpless to prevent him from jilting her in favour of a real princess. In despair, she threw herself into the sea and turned to foam. . .

THE ROMANTIC PRESENT—pastimes for lovers. . .

Copenhagen is a city for strolling and shopping in, particularly with its mile-long traffic-free shopping route, which begins at the Town Hall Square (Rådhuspladsen) and ends at Kongens Nytorv. The variety of shops and elegant boutiques and cafés provides a relaxing way of wandering around the city. This is the place to look for souvenirs: for example, Danish knitwear, glass, stainless steel and china.

For those who enjoy taking things at a slow pace, why not go on one of the sightseeing boat tours which leave regularly from the harbour? To the south of the city, the island of **Amager** is a sight not to be missed! Much of the island was settled on by Dutch market gardeners, and they brought their own customs and costumes— indeed, the village of **Dragor** has remained virtually unchanged, with its narrow cobbled streets and pretty, quaint cottages.

On your walk around the city, head for the harbour bridge and turn left—here you will find **Amalienborg Plads**, an elegant square surrounded by four mansions which, in 1794, became the royal palaces. The changing of the guard can be seen every day at noon!

On the same side of the canal look out for the 1624 **Stock Exchange** building with its copper spire formed by the twisted tails of four dragons!

Also well worth a visit are the **Tivoli Gardens**, where you can combine scenic views with all the fun of the fair!

Copenhagen has been described as the cultural centre of Denmark, and it is perfect for romantic evenings out! There are plenty of theatres to choose from, and the Zealand Symphony Orchestra gives concerts in the **concert hall** at Tivoli. There are also several bars and a variety of jazz clubs for those who prefer a more energetic night out—perhaps your visit to Copenhagen will coincide with the annual jazz festival, which gives both Danish and foreign musicians a chance to show off their talents!

For lovers who enjoy a traditional candle-lit dinner, Copenhagen is the place to be! Choose from simple but delicious fare served in small, out-of-the-way cafés or some of the more up-market restaurants. Traditional dishes include *frikadeller*—meatballs made of pork—or *medisterpølse*, which is a type of grilled sausage. Denmark is also famous for its abundance of fish—try grilled plaice, trout, Greenland prawns or smoked salmon. Meals are often finished with cheese (Danish *ost*) and a popular drink is light beer—*øl*—such as that produced by the Carlsberg and Tuborg breweries in Copenhagen! Another typical Danish drink often had after dinner is *akvavit*—an aromatic brandy prepared with spices—but beware . . . it has a minimum alcohol content of 38%!

DID YOU KNOW THAT. . .?

* Copenhagen has a **population** of about 1 million, and as a whole Denmark is a country of which around 10% is covered by woodland.

* the Danish flag is known as the **Dannebrog** (Danish brog is colourful cloth). It comprises a white cross on a red background and, according to legend, fell from heaven in 1219!

* the Danish **alphabet** has three extra letters—Æ, Ø and Å.

* the way to say 'I love you' in Danish is '*Jeg elsker dig*'.

POSTCARDS FROM EUROPE

HARLEQUIN PRESENTS®

Hi!

I should be on cloud nine. Rolf Felder asked me to marry him. He's the handsome owner of a hotel chain here in Switzerland, but I'm not convinced he'll ever view our marriage as anything more than one of convenience. I'm desperately in love with him—what should I do?   Love, Abigail

Travel across Europe in 1994 with Harlequin Presents. Collect a new Postcards From Europe title each month!

Don't miss
NO PROMISE OF LOVE
by Lilian Peake
Harlequin Presents #1700

Available in November wherever Harlequin Presents books are sold.

HPPFE11

Relive the romance.... This December,
Harlequin and Silhouette are proud to bring you

by Request™

Little Matchmakers

All they want for Christmas is a mom *and* a dad!

Three complete novels by your favorite authors—
in one special collection!

THE MATCHMAKERS by Debbie Macomber
MRS. SCROOGE by Barbara Bretton
A CAROL CHRISTMAS by Muriel Jensen

When your child's a determined little matchmaker,
anything can happen—especially at Christmas!

Available wherever
Harlequin and Silhouette books are sold.

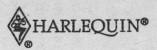

HARLEQUIN® Silhouette®